MY BIG GREEN ALIEN ORC

STARLIGHT MONSTERS
BOOK 1

SKYE MACKINNON

Peryton Press

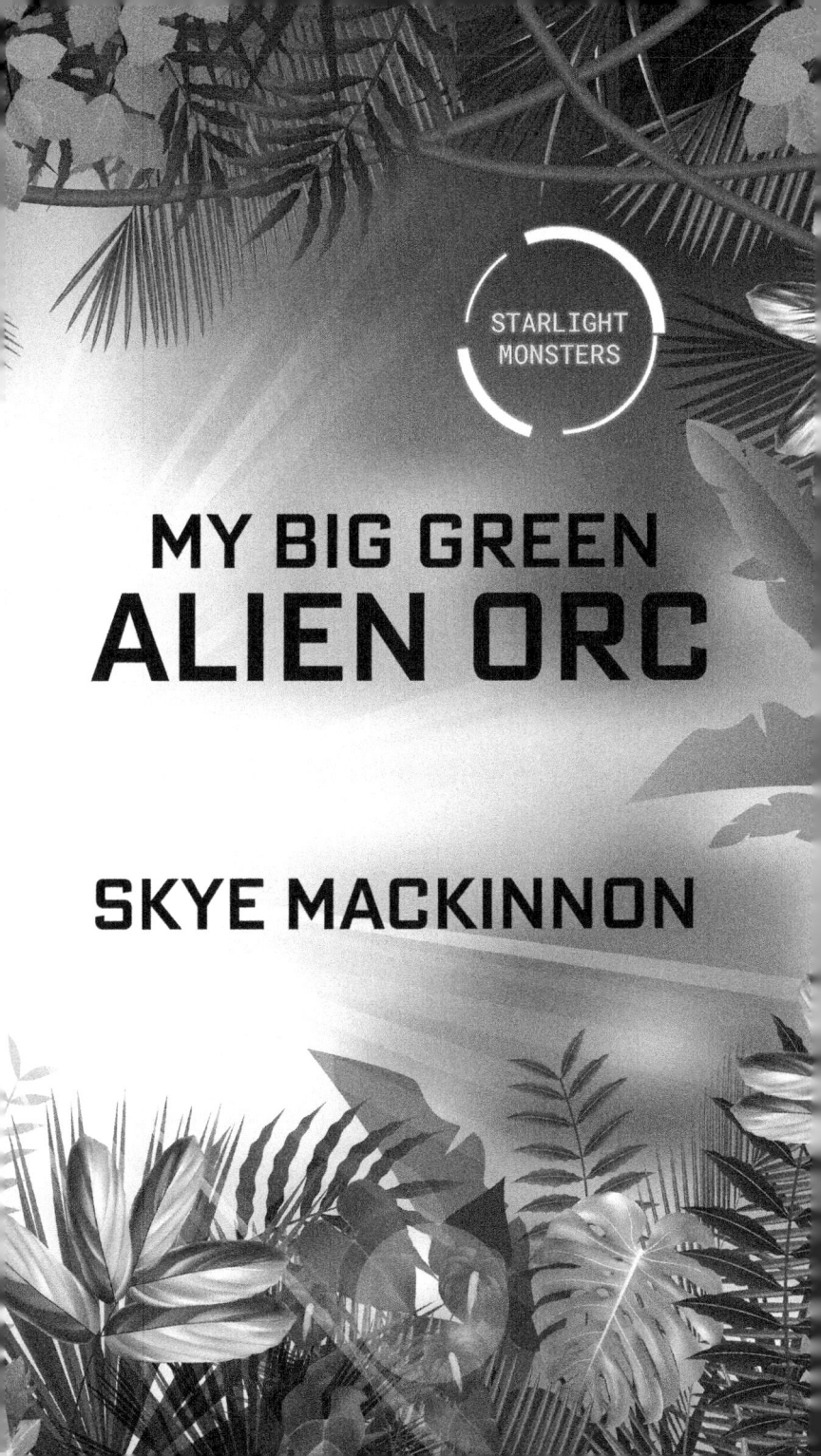

Copyright © 2022 by Skye MacKinnon

All rights reserved.

No part of this book may be reproduced in any form or by any electronic or mechanical means, including information storage and retrieval systems, without written permission from the author, except for the use of brief quotations in a book review.

Cover by Gombar Cover Designs

Published by Peryton Press

perytonpress.com

CONTENTS

Prologue	9
1. Fay	13
2. Vruhag	23
3. Fay	33
4. Vruhag	41
5. Fay	49
Chirpy	59
6. Vruhag	61
7. Fay	71
8. Vruhag	79
9. Fay	87
10. Vruhag	95
11. Fay	103
12. Vruhag	113
13. Fay	125
14. Vruhag	135
15. Fay	145
16. Vruhag	155
17. Fay	167
18. Vruhag	177
19. Fay	187
20. Vruhag	199
21. Fay	207
22. Vruhag	215
Epilogue	225
Acknowledgments	231
The Starlight Universe	233
About the Author	235
Also By	237

To all my furry fluffballs, past and present, who together inspired the chii

PROLOGUE
VRUHAG

I can smell *her*.

There's no doubt about it.

She's close.

Her scent is mixed with that of blood. Hers? Someone else's?

I throw myself against the bars again. They shake but don't budge. Few materials in the universe can withstand a full-blooded orc in battle rage, but this cell is orc-proof from top to bottom. I've spent the past three cycles trying to find a way out. My body aches, and I'm covered in half-healed bruises.

I'm trapped. And now my mate is here.

I push my nose through a gap in the bars, breathe in deep. Her scent makes my tusks throb. My shaft presses against its protective casing.

I need to see her. Touch her. Claim her.

I fight against the mating fever, but it's too late. The moment her scent entered my nostrils, I was lost.

"Mate!" I yell as loud as I can.

Other prisoners heckle and jeer. I listen for a response from her, but none comes.

I curl my fingers around the metal bars.

She's out there. Close.

I need to find her before the madness takes me.

1
FAY

The mother of all hangovers drummed against my temples. I sat up, only for nausea to make my stomach vault. I pressed my lips together, fighting the urge to vomit. I'd clearly drunk too much last night, even though I couldn't remember going out. I groaned and tried to recall how I got into this state. I'd gone for a walk in the dark, trying to clear my head after a long day at work. Then, nothing.

Had I met a friend and gone partying? Unlikely, but if my headache was anything to go by, it must have been a long, alcohol-fuelled night. I'd not had one of those in years. Now I was going to have to pay the price.

I fumbled for the nightlight, but my fingers only met cold metal. I froze. My little cat-shaped light was on the bedside table to my right; it always was. There shouldn't be anything metal there. Come to think of it, I didn't see the usual dim glow of the streetlight coming through my curtains either. I liked to sleep in the dark, but even my blackout curtains couldn't dispel all the light from that blasted lamp. I'd written to the council about it many times.

I felt around me, touching the duvet, which turned out to be just a silky blanket, not the thick lambswool duvet I usually slept under.

I wasn't in my bed. I wasn't home.

Maybe a friend's place. Had to be. I'd had too much to drink and crashed at theirs. Or had I gone home with a guy? Unlikely. Those days were long gone. I'd not been with a man in so long that I might as well call myself a virgin again. Dry spell? Sahara Desert, more like it.

I needed light. Where was my phone? Not in my pockets. I was still wearing jeans and a shapeless merino wool jumper. Not exactly party clothes. And no phone. I'd had a shoulder bag; I remembered putting my keys in it as well as a box of biscuits (one should never leave the house without snacks).

It was no good. I'd have to feel my way around and hope I wouldn't stumble over things or step on used condoms. Although the fact that I was still wearing jeans spoke against that theory.

As a first surprise, the floor was much closer than I expected. I wasn't on a bed, just on a mattress surrounded by a steel frame to keep it in place.

I walked slowly, arms extended. Two steps, three, four. My hands hit a cold wall. Colder than it should have been. It was smooth and glossy. Marble, maybe.

I felt my way along the wall, around a corner, then another. No shelves, no windows, no doors, just smooth stone.

My naked toes bumped against something hard. I sucked in a sharp breath as pain shot through my foot and up my leg. Ouch. I bent down to feel for whatever was in the way. A square cube, maybe two feet high and wide, with a hole in the centre. Some sort of container?

I reached into the hole. My fingers broke through cold water. Not just cold, *icy*, almost frozen. A shiver ran down my back, and I quickly pulled back. Weird.

I still had no light nor a door. Maybe it was time to find out whose room this was.

"Hello?" I called out. The stone walls swallowed my voice, absorbing the sound. I'd once been in an anechoic chamber at a science museum. It was so quiet that my heartbeat and breathing were the only sound. This was similar. Not quite as intense, but now that I focused on it, yes, I thought I could hear my elevated heartbeat. Who had a semi-anechoic chamber at home?

I shrugged off the anxiety breaking through my barriers. This was strange, but not scary. I'd dealt with worse situations. Much, much worse. That time when I came under fire in Afghanistan. Without my military escort, I may not have survived.

This was nothing. Just a strange room and a hangover.

I was a tough cookie. At least, I had been until I

took a desk job to lick my wounds and pretend to be normal. Now, the old Fay had to make an appearance.

"Hello!" I yelled, but once again, the sound of my voice was absorbed by the walls. I doubted anyone outside the room would have even heard a whisper. A shiver ran down my back, and it wasn't because of the cold.

I continued my exploration. By the time I almost stumbled over the mattress, it was getting harder to stay optimistic. No door. No windows. This wasn't the room of some guy I'd picked up in a club.

This was a prison cell.

In darkness, time passes strangely.

I wore a watch, but it was an old-fashioned one without a backlight. Not a fancy fitness tracker. Now I wished I'd splashed out on one. I missed my phone terribly. Nomophobia was real. I was always on my phone. Always texting, always scrolling through the news, always checking my emails. I'd not been without a phone in my hand since... well, when had smart-phones been invented?

I tried to sleep to pass the time, but that quickly turned out to be impossible. I wasn't tired, my head hurt and anxious thoughts drifted through my mind. There was no way I could sleep like that.

To occupy myself, I walked around the room, exploring the walls with my hands. I reached up as high as I could, then tried the opposite and explored the lower part of the walls while kneeling. No door. No opening at all.

The ceiling could have been just out of reach or five metres above me. I had no way to know. There had to be a ceiling, though, otherwise I'd see light or feel a draught.

I hated not knowing where I was. I hated not knowing what time it was. And most of all, I hated the theories popping into my head.

Abducted by terrorists. It wouldn't be the first time. But there had been no communication. No demands. No torture.

A psychological experiment run by the government. Unlikely.

A dream. Or a coma. This could all be just in my mind.

Again, unlikely. It felt real. My toes still throbbed from when I bumped against the stone cube.

Aliens.

I snorted at that thought. Sure, why not. It would be the scoop of the century. I'd either get every journalism prize there was, or end up sectioned. I grinned as I imagined the headline.

Interview with an Extraterrestrial.

No, I didn't believe in aliens, at least not in the little green men variety. Microbes surviving on distant planets, sure. But sentient beings? No way. They would have contacted - or obliterated - Earth long ago. We would have noticed. Or would have *been* noticed, considering how many satellites now circled our planet. We made a lot of noise for a species that had barely reached its own moon.

I returned to the bed and wrapped my arms around my knees. I didn't like showing weakness, but right now, I was alone. No one could see me.

Or could they? There could be night vision cameras attached to the ceiling. I tensed and glared into the darkness, just in case.

"If this is some sort of joke, I'm going to make sure to destroy you," I said. My voice was a little hoarse, but it helped make me sound more threatening. "I'm going to ruin your reputation. I'm going to spread every nasty rumour I can think of. I've dealt with worse people than you. Trust me, you don't scare me. You should be scared of me."

It made me feel a little better. I doubt anyone was listening to me, but still, it was good to show strength.

"Weakness is for pussies." Dan's voice rang in my head. "You might have one, but you aren't one."

He used to say that all the time. I couldn't help but smile at the memory. He'd been the toughest man I'd ever met. If he hadn't got himself blown to pieces, I may have considered moving in with him.

Dan. Such a waste. My smile wavered. It had been three years, but it still hurt.

The floor shook. An earthquake. Fuck. I was trapped in this room and I couldn't get to a safe space outside. If the ceiling collapsed, I was toast. There wasn't even a table to seek shelter under.

I rushed to the closest wall and pressed against it. Except that the wall moved as soon as I touched it, sliding upwards. Light burst into the room from underneath, so bright I had to squeeze my eyes shut. The floor continued to shake violently. I sank to my knees while trying to peek through the gap where the walls used to be.

Were the walls being lifted or was the floor sinking? Either way, I was no longer trapped. If only the light wasn't so bright. I still couldn't see anything.

Maybe that was on purpose. Someone didn't want me to look beyond my strange prison cell.

I struggled to my feet. The shaking wasn't getting any less, but I had to see what was going on. This might be my only chance to escape. Who knew when the walls were going to come down again. Or the floor back up. By now, it almost felt as if both the walls were going up and the floor was moving down at the same time. I was disoriented, and the glaring light wasn't making it any better.

Bright spotlights or something similar were directed at me from all sides. After being kept in the dark, I should have been grateful for the light, but I wasn't. It was just as bad. At least I could finally see the inside of the room, even though the glaring light was blinding me, making it hard to take in the details. The silky blanket on the bed reflected the light, shimmering silver with a tint of blue. Not how I'd pictured it at all. The cube I'd bumped my toes on was exactly the same metallic silver, although the liquid inside was bright green. It looked like nothing I'd ever seen. Something you'd find in the cauldron of a witch, maybe. Some strange piece of art?

"KAWUUM BARUUM DI KALUUMBU."

A voice boomed from all around me, so loud I instinctively covered my ears. The language was not one I recognised, and it was loud, so bloody loud. Together with the blinding light, my senses were being overwhelmed so much that it hurt.

"KSUUBU AU BARUM FAY MACHALIN. KAWUUM."

I ripped my hands off my ears when I heard my name. Fay MacLean. Booming Voice was talking about me. They *knew* me.

Without warning, a searing heat erupted all over my body. I screamed in pain, but it was over in less than a second. Cool air touched my skin, soothing the burn.

I looked down at myself and wanted to scream all over again.

My clothes had disappeared and I was now entirely naked.

2
VRUHAG

I killed three guards before they managed to close the collar around my neck. As soon as it snapped shut, a searing pain ran down my spine, making my legs collapse under me. I crumpled to the floor while the guards jeered and laughed.

They were going to suffer. As soon as I got out of here and rescued my mate, I was going to kill them all. Slowly. Taking them apart piece by piece. They would regret attacking my ship and abducting me every painful click until the moment they'd die. And then I would mutilate their corpses and feed them to my hyggena. My beasts would be hungry after my long absence.

They dragged me backwards and propped me against a wall. With the collar doing something to my spine, I couldn't move. Even snarling at them was almost impossible.

A drone floated into the cell, expanding into a large screen.

The guards left, grunting foul insults as they did, then shut the door, leaving me alone. The collar was still active, forcing me to stay in place and look at the screen. Some sort of torture, most likely. It flickered to life, showing a small figure in a sea of light.

The camera zoomed closer, exposing the figure as a female. She stood on a platform, resembling a version of my cell with the same sort of bed and pisspot, but much smaller. The female wavered on her feet, clearly unsteady, but she managed to stay standing. She blinked into the light, unaware of the drones circling the hovering platform, of the crowd in the distance.

Even though I only saw her on the screen, I knew it deep within my heart. She was mine. My mate. The female I'd scented.

"Welcome to the Trials of Kalumbu."

The announcement stole my breath.

Kalumbu. Of all the cursed places in this universe. Now it all made sense. Why I was brought to this cell without a word, without a reason for the attack of my ship. Why I could smell my mate.

Kalumbu. This planet has made people rich. It's changed lives. But most of all, it takes lives. A thousand deaths every rotation. It is said that the plants in the planet's jungle can no longer survive without blood.

"The bride is Fay Machalin. Welcome her."

The shouts of hundreds of spectators echoed the

announcer's dramatic voice. They'd paid exorbitant amounts of credits to be here, to witness the Trials in person. Billions more would watch via the black channels on their ships, in their homes. It was illegal to even view the Trials on most civilised planets, but when have laws ever stopped anyone.

The female - *my* female - turned back and forth on the platform, as if trying to decide what to do. She must not have realised yet that this was Kalumbu. If she'd even heard of the Trials. The show's audience fell among the very rich – who'd increase their wealth by betting on contestants – and the very poor – who for once could feel like they had it better than the poor sods dying in the Trials. Middle-class society either ignored Kalumbu or had no knowledge of it. I hoped my mate fell into that category. I wanted her to have grown up safe and happy, without the taint of poverty or the arrogance of wealth.

Three of the circling drones shot bright rays at the female. She cried as her clothing dissolved, leaving her naked. I growled, fury filling every cell of my body. They were humiliating her.

I didn't recognise her species. She was tiny, pale and at first glance lacked any natural defences. Two arms, two legs, no tail, no horns. Her pink skin looked soft and vulnerable. Not a single scale in sight. As much as I craved running my claws over her skin, test just how soft it was, right now scales or armoured plates would have served her better. Her auburn mane was tied into a knot, making it hard to see how long it was. I hoped that she had hidden talons or at least some poisonous fangs. Without them, she'd be dead within ten clicks of the Trials.

"You may not have seen a specimen like this before," the announcer boomed, sounding excited. "This is a rare Peritan from the planet Peritus. They only recently discovered spaceflight and think they're alone in the universe."

Roaring laughter followed his words. It only made me angrier. They'd abducted a female from some primitive backwater planet. She wouldn't have any experience in dealing with aliens. She wouldn't even have a universal translator implant. That would explain her confusion. If she knew what was going on, she'd be terrified. Instead, she slowly made her way to the edge of the platform, curiosity mirroring on her fine features. I found it surprisingly easy to read her emotions. Her mimic was not unlike that of my own species, even though she was so much daintier.

I wondered what Peritan males looked like. They had to be enormous to be able to take care of their vulnerable females. Did she have a male? Was there someone waiting for her back on her planet?

That thought made me even angrier.

She was *mine*.

A drone zooms down to the edge of the platform, blocking her way. I assumed there were other safeguards to prevent people from throwing themselves off.

It would be a quick death compared to what awaited her.

What awaited us.

I'd watched the Trials often enough to know what was about to happen. Yet seeing a large drone swoop down and pick up my mate in its spindly metal arms broke my heart.

I'd never make it to her in time. She was too fragile. They'd even removed her clothing. They hadn't given her a weapon, which meant nobody had claimed her as her sponsor. Her blood was going to water the jungle, yet one more forgotten victim of this cursed entertainment industry.

While I watched the drone carry her away into the distance, I tried to remember the times I'd watched the Trials of Kalumbu. I'd been young, brazen, arrogant. Watching people die without showing emotion had been a test of my strength. Or so I'd thought. I'd been an idiot, trying to impress females that weren't my mate. But if I hadn't, I would be in an even worse situation. I'd be going into this blind, while at least now I had an idea of what was about to happen.

They'd had weak females before, always paired with an especially strong male. In any other situation, this would have flattered me. But how often did these females survive? I couldn't remember a single time. And whenever the female perished, her mate would go insane, becoming the most effective weapon in the Trials. They had nothing to lose. They were willing to take the other contestants into the abyss.

That was my fate. If my female died, the madness would take over. No orc could survive long without his mate. I may not have seen her in person, may not have touched her, but her scent had activated the process. We were bound together now, our fates entwined. And if she died, I would kill anyone and everything that got in my way. I would fight and murder and destroy until someone stronger ended my life.

I was a dead orc walking. There was no way either of us was going to survive this.

The screen flickered off before I could see where they were taking my mate. She could have been anywhere on the planet.

A guard entered the cell, his three tails curled around his waist. "Your sponsor offers you one weapon of your choice. What do you choose?"

The collar wasn't letting me speak. I glared at the guard. He must have been aware of my predicament. And yes, the ugly grin spreading across his scarred face was proof that he knew.

"You don't choose a weapon? Such a pity. You will have to fight unarmed."

"Klet, that's against the rules," someone drawled from outside my cell. "We'll all be disciplined if they find out."

"I'm not going to switch off his collar," Klet grunted. "Did you see what he did to the others?"

He pulled his axe from his belt and threw it on the floor in front of me. "That'll have to do. It's not like he'll make it for long anyway."

He gave me a nasty grin before leaving the cell, locking the door behind him. The drone and its screen had disappeared, taking away any chance of distraction. Now all I could do was sit and worry about what my mate was facing at this very moment. Had she been dropped on the planet's surface yet? Was she injured?

She wasn't dead. I'd know. I'd feel it.

Already, the madness was scratching at the edges of my mind. I needed to get to her before it was too late.

The cell shook and the lights turned dark. The collar vibrated and with a flash of pain, it sprung open. I ripped it off my neck and threw it to the other side of the cell.

My limbs felt weak. Pins and needles ran over my skin, and when I gripped the axe, I almost let it drop again. I sat back against the wall, gathering my strength. I was too weak for the Trials. I'd not eaten or drunk in days.

I cursed the guards who'd tortured me in every language I knew.

"May your mother's crotch wither and pull you back into its shrivelled womb." That was Old Tangaeitean, one of my favourites. I only knew a few choice curses in it, but every single one of them was superb in its vulgarity.

The walls lifted, blinding light taking their place. I squinted into the light as my name echoed through speakers all around me. I ignored the announcer, ignored the camera drones, ignored everything. Instead, I focused on the bond that connected me to my mate.

Faint, barely perceptible, yet it was there, in my heart. I was connected to her and I'd find her.

The platform trembled as I was transported down to the surface. I didn't know what awaited me there, but I didn't have a choice. I would have to fight, kill, survive in order to get to my mate and make sure she was safe.

3
FAY

Icy water woke me. It entered my mouth, pushed against my skin. I flailed my limbs, trying to get control over my body. A light above me signalled the water's surface. I swam, drawing on every spark of energy I possessed. The freezing cold made me sluggish. At least I wore no clothes to weigh me down.

When I broke through the surface, I gasped for air. It was warm and humid as if I'd been thrown into a greenhouse. A strange smell hung in the air, heavy like flowery perfume. I turned slowly, looking at my surroundings. The last I remembered was a metal spider-like machine grabbing me. Then my ears had popped and everything went dark.

I was swimming in a small lake framed by giant trees that seemed to reach all the way into the sky. I'd never seen trees that tall before. It seemed impossible for them to stay upright. Their bark was shades of purple and blue, glistening in the light of the sun.

This wasn't Earth. There was no other explanation.

I was on an alien planet. Or in a dream or in a coma, but I actually preferred being on an alien planet. I didn't know why I found it easier to deal with than the alternative.

I turned onto my back. The view proved that this wasn't Earth. Two large moons hung in the sky, while a blinding white sun shone in between them. A few puffy clouds floated in the wind high above, but even they didn't look like the clouds I was used to.

The cold seeping into my bones reminded me that I had to get out of the water. I stayed on my back to conserve energy and slowly made my way to the closest bank of the lake. By the time I dragged my sore body onto dry land, I'd lost all feeling in my fingers and toes. My teeth chattered loudly.

I focussed on the sounds around me. Squawking in the canopy made me think of birds. Hopefully cute, harmless parrots, not some man-eating monsters. A low buzz reminded me of insects, although I couldn't see any. But I shouldn't assume that the fauna here was anything like what I was used to. It would have been strange if animals here evolved the same way as they did on Earth. For all I knew, the insects on this planet were sentient beings, while the birds had multiple wings and were carnivores.

A shiver ran down my back, and it wasn't just because of the cold.

I was being watched. I felt it in my bones. Someone - or something - was watching me. The undergrowth was too thick to see far. Anything could lurk behind the purple grass and the indigo leaves.

Think, Fay. You've been dropped into hostile territory. What do you do next?

My teeth were chattering so much that my jaw was starting to hurt. I needed to get warm. Clothes. Shelter. A weapon against whoever or whatever was watching me.

I hated carrying weapons. I knew how to shoot a gun; I'd got lessons before going on my first assignment in a crisis region, but I'd never enjoyed it. It was hypocritical, I knew, relying on armed soldiers or guards for protection and being okay with them shooting others if necessary. It wasn't that I didn't want to get my hands dirty. I just didn't like the feeling of carrying something that could end someone else's life in an instant.

This wasn't the time to think about the past. I needed to act now. I didn't know how long the days were on this planet. I might only have an hour until night time and I didn't want to still be naked and exposed then.

I slowly made my way along the bank of the lake, scanning the undergrowth until I found a large bush with massive leaves. They were perfectly square, unlike any plant I'd ever seen. I didn't know nature produced square shapes. I pulled off one and wrapped it around my waist. It was just big enough to act as a skirt. A piece of leaf broke off when I tried to twist it like a bath towel to ensure that it stayed put around my hips.

I needed a belt. All around me, thick vines hung

from the branches high above. They would have made perfect ropes, but they looked too strong to pull apart without a knife. Oh well, there was no harm in trying.

I grabbed the closest with both hands and pulled as hard as I could. Just like I'd expected, it didn't come loose. It barely budged. Tarzan would've been able to climb up the vines and hide in the canopy, but it was months since I'd last set foot into a gym. I wished I was some kind of action hero instead of the desk-bound journalist I'd become.

I'd have to make do with what I had. I ripped one leaf into long strips, but when I tried to knot them together, once again they crumbled into pieces. How strange. The leaves looked stronger than they really were.

"Fuck!"

I threw the leaves back on the ground. Even nature had conspired against me.

My bare foot touched something soft. I stepped back, revealing a patch of bright yellow moss. I experimentally pulled some of it off the ground. It easily gave way. Hidden beneath fallen leaves and roots was yet more moss and soon, I was left with a large piece of it. It was stretchy and soft, much more suited to making some clothes than the purple leaves.

I wrapped the moss around my body like a beach wrap, knotting it at the top. It was crazy how soft it felt against my skin. I would have loved to have a mattress made of this stuff. For a moment, I considered building a shelter here, but my instincts were telling me to press on.

I quickly wrapped some more moss around my feet as makeshift shoes. They wouldn't protect me from sharp stones, but it might be better than staying barefoot.

It was strange what difference clothes could make. I no longer felt as exposed and vulnerable now that my nakedness was no longer on full display. The prickling at the back of my neck was still there, however. Someone was watching me.

I forced myself to ignore the uneasiness and continued my search for a place to shelter. My feet hurt from the uneven ground, but at least walking in combination with my new moss dress had made me warm again. No more chattering teeth.

A wet patch on a smooth rock made me stop. This was where I'd climbed out of the water. I'd walked all around the lake and hadn't seen anything resembling a path that would make it easier to explore the dense jungle. All I had to show for my efforts was the moss. No weapon, no food, no shelter. I clearly needed to up my game.

But it wasn't a *game*. This was real. I was stranded on an alien planet and until I figured out how I got here, who put me here and how to get back home, I had to survive. By myself. No soldiers to guard me. No local experts to show me around. No satellite phone to call for help.

Just me.

The enormity of the situation made me want to cry.

Until today, I'd thought that I was a strong person who could handle anything.

Turns out I wasn't.

A rustle in the undergrowth to my left caused me to whirl around. I half expected a monstrous predator to walk out of the jungle, but no, there was nothing. Some of the leaves trembled slightly, but that may have just been the wind.

I grabbed a rock from the ground, gripping it tightly. Better than nothing.

One of the purple leaves dipped down, pulled by something.

This wasn't the wind. Something was hiding in the bush.

I took a step back until the heel of my foot hit icy water. There was nowhere to run. I bet whatever predators roamed this planet were faster than me. I could've gone back into the lake, swum towards the centre, but I wouldn't survive the freezing cold for long.

I was so screwed.

More movement in the bushes. It was as if whatever was hiding there was teasing me. Revelling in my fear.

I was about ready to jump into the lake after all. Drowning seemed a whole lot nicer than being torn apart by alien beasts.

One of the leaves was pushed aside and three bright golden eyes stared at me.

4
VRUHAG

I burst from my cage and breathed in the humid jungle air, tasting it for any trace of my mate's scent. How long had it been since she'd arrived on the planet's surface? I'd passed out in transit and had lost track of time.

In the back of my mind, I automatically categorised the scents. Prey, predator or unfamiliar. On my home planet, I was close to the top of the food chain, with only a few beasts strong or clever enough to take on an orc. Here, on Kalumbu, I was prey. I'd watched stronger beings than me get eaten by the beasts that roamed this planet. It's why they'd chosen Kalumbu as the setting for the Trials. It was a beautiful planet, full of lush jungle and plants painted in colours we didn't even have names for on Orcadia. Yet almost everything here was deadly. Not just the beasts. The plants, too. I had watched a carnivorous flower devour a battle-hardened Ferven warrior as if he was nothing but an insect.

Kalumbu was going to kill me. It was just waiting for the right moment.

I tightened my grip on the axe the guard had given me. It was decently balanced, although I missed the feel of my own axe, passed down to me from my grandsire's mother, the strongest orcess ever seen. Her blood ran in my veins. I just hoped it would be enough to save my mate and myself.

"Ancestors protect me," I muttered and raised my fist to my forehead in sacred gesture.

They'd put a strange kilt-like garment on me while I was asleep, long leather straps attached to a belt that sat tightly against my hips. My feet and chest remained bare. I took one of the straps and tied it into a sling, turning it into a makeshift holder for the axe's hilt. Now I had my hands free, ready to fight.

Without my mate's scent, I had no idea where to go. They'd dropped me in a small clearing, surrounded by trees so high I could barely see their crowns. I could smell dozens of animals, but they were staying out of sight. If there were predators nearby, I couldn't sense them.

I needed to get a better idea of where on the planet they'd transported me to. I was glad now that I'd watched the Trials in the past. It gave me an advantage. I knew that Kalumbu was ninety per cent land covered in thick jungle, with the rest a small ocean near the South pole. There were long rivers that spanned almost the entire globe, so wide there was no way I'd be able to cross them. I could only hope that I could reach my mate on foot without having to build a raft.

Surely, they would not make it impossible for us to find each other. It was rare for both the male and the female to survive the Trials, but there always had to be the chance for it all to have a happy end. Most viewers tuned into the programme for the blood, death and despair, but from time to time, a couple found each other and survived for the necessary ten rotations. Only then were they transported off the planet's surface and taken to safety.

There was hope. Others have survived. Maybe we could, too. There was hope.

I whispered the words over and over again like a mantra. I could not give up before the Trials had even started properly.

I chose a tree and started the long climb up. It was the only way to orient myself.

My muscles ached after only a few minutes. Before my abduction, I'd been in good shape, training every day, but clinging to the tree strained my muscles in a way my usual exercises did not. Plus I'd had neither water nor food in days. I was used to hardship and rationing, but going without any sustenance was taking its toll.

I visualised my mate's face. Her pale skin, her long dark tresses, her confused yet angry expression when they'd dematerialised her clothes. There'd been a trace of fear, but she hadn't been paralysed by it. She was a strong female, I knew that already. But would she be strong enough to survive until I could get to her?

My right hand landed on something soft and squishy. I froze, my senses going on high alert. Did I touch an animal? A poisonous mushroom? An acid-laden flower?

I waited for pain to spread through my hand and arm. I'd seen it happen to other contestants. They touched some plant and dissolved into dust moments later.

But nothing happened. I climbed up a little higher, more careful this time where I put my hands, until I saw what I just touched. A patch of deep blue lichen. Harmless. Unless there was going to be a delayed reaction to it. Let's hope not. I wanted to be lucky for once. Finding one of the few plants on this planet that weren't lethal.

I continued my climb, but slower, hesitating each time before I grasped the thick scales of bark covering the tree. My body was aching all over. My muscles were screaming at me to stop and take a break, but the thought of my mate drove me on. She could be fighting for her life just now.

Sweat covered my palms and dripped down my forehead. Not much longer. The tree couldn't go on forever. Was it getting lighter? Was I imagining it?

A flock of birds lifted off the branches above me, making leaves and tiny bits of bark rain down on me. They cawed angrily, but again I was lucky and they didn't attack. I only got glimpses of the birds' bright colours through the thick canopy, but it was enough to know that they weren't some of the flesh-eating avians that I knew ruled the skies of Kalumbu.

By the time I finally reached the crown of the tree, my arms and legs were shaking with exhaustion. I could barely hang on any longer.

Four thick branches grew out of the top of the trunk in perfect symmetry to each other. I heaved myself onto the crotch where they merged, wide enough to accommodate my tired self. It felt good to sit.

The leaves here were much smaller and I finally had the view I'd been hoping for. I'd instinctively picked one of the tallest trees, letting me see almost uninterrupted in all directions. A sea of trees, their leaves shimmering all the colours of the rainbow, lay around me. They stood so close to each other that it looked like an uninterrupted surface, almost like a hilly landscape. There seemed no pattern to the colours, just a random assortment ranging from the faintest yellow to the deepest blue that reminded me of blood. Not my blood, orc blood was emerald green, but that of kringers, the feral beasts roaming the lands I grew up in. Hunting them was traditional training for all young orcs. I'd killed hundreds of them with weapons, my hands and even my feet, back when I practised the ancient martial art of Hung'do.

As beautiful as the view was, it also drained the last drop of hope that I might find my mate soon. The trees were endless, not a single gap in the canopy. There were no distinguishing features that would help me find my way, just trees and more trees. If there were rivers crossing the landscape, they were so small that they didn't create a gap in the forest's roof.

Far in the distance, a flock of birds was flying against the wind. In my direction. I didn't want to wait to find out if they were the flesh-eating kind. With one last look at the stunning sea of trees, I started my long climb down.

The descent took the last of my energy reserves and by the time I was finally back on solid ground, my legs were trembling with exhaustion. My palms were torn and bloody from the rough bark. I'd have to wash off the blood before it attracted a predator.

I drew in a deep breath of air, smelling for water. There was the faintest trace to the West. With no idea where my mate was, it was as good a direction as any to take.

I walked as quickly as my tired limbs allowed. The ground was uneven and I kept getting caught in roots and brambles. Thorns scratched my bare ankles and thighs. The soles of my feet were thick enough to protect me from stones and sharp pieces of wood, but would it be the same for my mate? I dimly remembered she'd worn wrappings around her feet before they'd dematerialised her clothes. I hoped that had been just a fashion thing and not because her species wasn't used to walking barefoot. It would make her even more vulnerable.

A growl broke from my throat at the thought of my helpless mate. My vengeance would be terrible. First, I had to find her, but once we were together, once she was safe, I'd make them pay. Every guard, every organiser, every sponsor, every viewer of the Trials. I'd tear out their throats and feast on their blood. I'd rip their insides to the outside and let their life drain away.

Battle rage clouded my vision as if fog was rising from the ground. The madness was starting. I had to focus. Fight the urge to give into my feral nature, turn into a beast.

I'd be of no use to my mate if I succumbed to the mating fever.

I had to survive ten rotations on Kalumbu.

But I wouldn't stay sane for more than three.

5
FAY

If a puppy, a kitten and a baby rabbit were mashed into one, the result would still be nowhere near as heart-tinglingly cute as the little beast staring at me. It reminded me of a golden monkey, except that it had three huge eyes, feathers instead of fur and two tails that were currently wrapped around the branches behind it. It was the size of a small cat and had the same kind of ears, with tiny golden tufts of fur – or were they feathers, too? – growing inside. Its face was elongated, ending in a pointy nose like a mouse's, with silver whiskers sprouting from its cheeks. I'd never seen anything cuter. It had to be the eyes, big and dark and watery. I wanted to cradle the little animal against my chest and never let it go.

It didn't move, only stared at me. Its front paws were grasping some thin branches that it had pushed aside. There was a certain intelligence in its gaze, an awareness, but I wasn't sure just how clever this beast was. Or if it was hostile. It didn't look it, but I was on an alien planet. I had no idea about the rules of this place. Everything that looked cute might be dangerous. I really should turn away and leave before it decided to attack. But I couldn't. The animal's gaze kept me trapped and I felt myself reaching out for it.

It watched me, unblinking, until my right hand was only an inch away from its front paws.

This was a bad idea. It could easily bite me and what then? The wound could get infected and game over. But I couldn't move. My heart pounded in my chest. I suddenly felt very aware of my nakedness. I was bare in front of this animal and it was *looking* at me. Into me. It seemed to peer into the depths of my soul.

It was appraising me. What would happen if I was found to be lacking?

I didn't know how long I stood there, one hand extended, frozen in the animal's judging gaze. With every second that passed, I felt more worthless. I wasn't a good person, at least not as good as I wanted to be. I'd made mistakes, tons of them. I'd hurt others. I'd hurt myself.

A deep sadness spread through my chest. I was failing the test. Something beautiful was just in reach, a golden light promising redemption, but I wasn't good enough.

What had I ever done in life that could be considered *good*?

I'd won prizes for my writing. So what? I'd earned

enough money to live comfortably. So what? I'd written about horrible events in faraway lands, gaining myself a reputation for courage and recklessness. So what?

Had I ever helped someone? Had my stories made a difference to anyone but myself?

One smiling, dirt-covered face appeared in my mind. Layla, a bright young girl who'd lost her leg in a landmine accident. One of my first feature stories had been about her. After my article had been published, donations had poured in, giving her parents the funds to buy a proper prosthesis and send her to a private rehabilitation centre. If I'd not written about her, would she have received the medical care she'd so desperately needed?

The image faded, leaving me looking into the alien creature's three eyes once more. Its pointy nose twitched, then it jumped. In a woosh of gold, it moved, faster than my eyes could register. It landed on my outstretched arm, its two tails wrapping around my wrist. Tiny claws dug into my skin, but it didn't seem to hurt me on purpose, it was just holding on a little too tightly.

Again, it looked up at me and this time, its gaze was warm and friendly, none of the judgement left. It chittered softly before climbing onto my shoulder, settling there. One tail wrapped around my neck, the other around my upper arm, until it was anchored in place.

"You're here to stay?" I asked it wryly.

It squeaked in response. The sound made my heart melt.

"Alright then. Don't suppose you know where I can find some food and shelter?"

It chittered animatedly, but I wasn't sure if it was actually responding or just making random animal sounds. How intelligent was this little beast? I was probably reading too much into its actions. It hadn't judged me. It had just looked at me to make sure I wasn't a threat. Right?

My wrist itched, exactly where it had been sitting. When I looked at my hand, a gasp broke from my lips. A golden ring was painted around my wrist, the same colour as the animal. I rubbed the mark, thinking it might be some kind of dust that it had attached to its tails, but the colour remained, staining my skin like a tattoo.

The mark wasn't completely even, not like a paintbrush had drawn it. Small lines marred the sides of the band, reminding me of the bushy fur of the alien monkey's tails.

"What have you done?" I asked it while still rubbing my wrist. "How is this possible?"

It chirped sweetly before pressing its tiny head against my cheek. An image of golden paint on my face flashed before my eyes and I reached for the animal, lifting it off my shoulder and holding it as far away from me as possible. It squeaked indignantly, but I ignored it for now. I inspected my upper arm, where one of the tails had been, but to my relief there was no trace of golden marks. Without a mirror, I couldn't know if my neck was also clean. How was I going to explain that strange tattoo when I got home?

Then it hit me. There was no guarantee I'd ever get home.

I was on an alien planet with no idea how I'd got here. Home could be light years away.

Nobody was going to come rescue me.

I was alone.

The animal chirped and wriggled in my grip. Well, not quite alone. With a sigh, I sat it back on my shoulder and immediately, it wrapped its tails around me once more. It clamped one paw around the top of my ear as if to make sure that I couldn't lift it off its perch again.

It seemed I was stuck with the little beast.

"Do you have a name?"

It chirped in response.

"Chirp? Chirpy? Guess it's as good as anything. I probably wouldn't be able to pronounce your alien name anyway. If your chirping is a language. Who knows, maybe you're the sentient species on this planet. Are you?"

Its huge dark eyes sparked with awareness, maybe intelligence, but I couldn't be sure.

Suddenly, a howl in the distance broke the silence. A shiver ran down my back while fear made my heart beat faster. It was the howl of a predator getting ready to chase his prey.

Chirpy tightened his grip on me, then chattered in a low tone, as if it was whispering.

"I wish I knew what you were saying," I sighed. "If you know of a safe place, now would be a good time to lead me there."

Chirp, chirp, chitter. Not helpful. But then it unfurled one of its tails from my neck and held it out like a straight rod, pointing to my left.

"Are you pointing?" I asked, not quite sure if I could believe my eyes. I'd read once that only primates and elephants could point, so what were the chances of this tiny alien animal having the same level of intelligence?

It chirped, sounding impatient. I turned in the direction the tail was pointing, and it adjusted the angle so that it now pointed straight ahead.

"I can't believe I'm doing this," I muttered as I began walking in the direction Chirpy was indicating. The undergrowth was slightly less thick here and I managed to walk more or less in a straight line, only occasionally circling trees. The soles of my feet hurt from sharp stones and branches and one of my moss foot wraps was unravelling, but the howls in the distance made me carry on without pause. When we got to a fallen tree trunk covered in pale orange moss, Chirpy moved its tail to two o'clock.

"Change of direction, eh?"

It wasn't as if I had anywhere else to go. I followed Chirpy's instructions, accompanied by blood-churning howls every few minutes. They weren't getting any closer, but I also wasn't getting further away from them.

The forest grew darker, the canopy so dense that

only a few sun rays found their way to the surface. Where they hit the mossy ground, flowers bloomed, interspersed by small mushrooms that seemed to compete with the flowers for sunlight. It didn't feel like the sun's position had changed much since I'd been dropped into the lake. Several hours must have passed, but it still felt like midday. How long were the days on this planet? I wish I knew more about space. Were there planets that didn't have night and day rhythms?

To be fair, I wasn't exactly looking forward to being in this forest at night, so having endless daylight didn't seem like a bad thing. Just...weird.

The ground was rising slowly and my breathing grew heavier. I was hungry, thirsty and tired. All I wanted was to be back home on my sofa. Having adventures was all good and well until you were in the middle of them, fighting for survival on an alien planet. I'd been in danger before, but I'd never been this alone. There'd always been the hope of a way out, an extraction plan, a satellite phone, a group of soldiers guarding my back.

"Weakness is for pussies." The memory of Dan's voice echoed through my mind. "You might have one, but you're not one."

"Thanks, Dan," I whispered. He was still helping me, even after death. He would have been good at this. I bet by now, he'd have already built a shelter, made food and befriended a local.

All I had done was meet an alien animal that was leading me who knew where. Hiking up this hill felt good, though. I might be able to get a view from the top. There might be a village or city I could go to. Since aliens had brought me to this planet, chances were they had permanent dwellings here. There had to be a point to it all. They wouldn't just kidnap me from Earth, transport me here and then drop me in the jungle to die. That didn't make sense. I assumed that space travel was expensive even for aliens. There had to be a reason. A purpose. I wasn't here to die.

Maybe it was an experiment to learn about humans. Maybe they were planning an invasion and wanted to know how humans reacted to challenges. It sounded like the plot of a bad sci-fi novel, not that I read those. I was more of a thriller and crime kind of person. Dan had made me watch Star Trek, but we'd never finished watching all the Star Wars films. He'd been blown up before we got to the end. I'd always planned to watch them by myself in his honour, but finishing would be too final. I wasn't ready for that yet.

Chirpy dug its claws into the ridge of my ear and I stopped, realising I'd been walking without paying attention to my surroundings. Bad idea. I had to focus.

Its tail unfurled and pointed at a large fallen boulder, framed by two trees with smooth purple bark. Their branches intertwined a few metres above the ground, making it appear like a huge door standing on the rock. Behind it, mist swirled in a single sunbeam piercing the canopy. The air seemed to sparkle. It looked magical; a portal into another world.

A howl sounded behind us, closer than before.

Another, then a third. Fuck. They were closing in. Whatever reason they'd had to keep their distance until now, it seemed they had decided to begin the hunt for good.

With a shriek, Chirpy jumped off my shoulder, landing on all fours, then ran towards the boulder. Its two tails were erect and curled around each other like a braid.

"Wait!" I shouted, but it was too late. Without looking back, Chirpy ran through the gap in the trees and disappeared in the glittering mist.

CHIRPY

6
VRUHAG

My diamond claws ripped through the beast's soft belly and its innards poured onto the ground with a squelch. I'd stalked my prey for over an hour, but now I'd finally cornered it. The smell of hot blood filled the air, alerting any nearby predator of my presence. I had to be quick. Foregoing thousands of years of evolution, I drew on the base predator within me and buried my snout in the beast's belly, ripping pieces of meat from bone and swallowing it raw. My sires would be appalled at my table manners.

I feasted as fast as I could, barely chewing the meat, very aware of how much noise I'd caused during the hunt. But I'd needed food to regain my strength. I was too wary to try any of the berries and mushrooms I'd come across, having seen the poisonous effects while watching the Trials. Assuming that everything on Kalumbu wanted to kill me was a good strategy to stay alive.

Once my hunger was sated, I left the remains of the beast on the forest floor. Maybe they'd distract any other predators from coming after me. I washed my hands and face in a little stream while praying to the ancestors that the water was clean. In one episode of the Trials, a contestant had melted from the inside out after drinking acidic water. I only took a few sips and waited a bit until I was sure it wasn't going to turn my insides into goo.

Watching the gurgling water of the stream made me sleepy. As much as my instincts were telling me to continue on and find my mate, I also knew that I had to rest. I wasn't in top form and I'd be of no use to my female if I was too weak to defend her. A few hours of sleep and I'd be good as new. Now that I'd had food and water, my metabolism would kick in. By the time I woke up, my energy levels would be refilled. Orcs were hardy, made for endurance, but captivity had depleted too many of my reserves.

Decision made, I took another large sip of refreshing water before heading away from the stream. Wildlife would come here frequently to drink, so it wasn't a safe place to linger. As much as I wanted to find a cosy cave, I didn't want to spend time searching for a den. No, climbing a tree was going to be the quicker option. It would be uncomfortable, but I'd learned to sleep in any position during my military training.

I made my way back into the depths of the forest, my senses on high alert, always on the lookout for both my mate and predators that could present a threat. I picked up a few old trails, but nothing fresh that would concern me. Some ancient bones, gnawed and stripped of all flesh, littered the forest floor. Animals or victims of the Trials? I didn't take a closer look.

For now, I was safe. It was unusual for the Trials. By now, I would have expected to be attacked. Instead, I'd been the one who'd done the hunting.

A horrible thought struck me. I was unharmed because the game makers' focus was on my mate. There'd been a pattern to the episodes of the Trials I'd watched. They'd concentrate on tormenting one of the contestants for a few hours, then switch to another. VIP subscribers could switch between cameras and watch all contestants at liberty, but the main Kalumbu channel was highly curated, only ever showing the most action-packed situations. And the death, naturally. That's what most people watched the show for. Pain, despair, death. It seemed to be a prime need of many species from across the universe to watch other beings suffer. I hated myself for having ever watched the show.

I balled my hands into fists. Claws pushed through my skin as rage filled me. My mate was in danger, yet I was powerless to protect her. I had to do something. But what? I didn't even know where she was. I'd never felt so weak.

The scent of blood hit my senses and an idea formed in my head. It was stupid, reckless, but it was better than doing nothing. Gone were all thoughts of sleep.

I could sleep when I was dead.

I prowled through the forest, following a faint trail. I was almost sure it was that of a predator. It *smelled* like predator. Hopefully it was going to be a big, dangerous beast. A challenge. Something that would look good on camera.

My plan was simple: Attract the game makers' attention. Distract from my mate. If I managed to start a fight with a deadly beast or two, it would make good entertainment. Viewers weren't used to that. Contestants may occasionally attack each other – unless they were mates, of course – but they never went searching for danger. They tried to survive rather than seek out their death. Only the most desperate, the ones who'd lost all hope after spending too long on the planet's surface, would voluntarily face one of Kalumbu's terrifying predators. And they did it to end their miserable lives.

I had no intention of dying. But I was prepared to get close to it to put on a show. I was prepared to get injured. There was no way I'd escape a battle with one of the beasts unscathed. I'd seen them, watched them tear contestants apart. Some were native to Kalumbu, evolved to be the ultimate predators in a hostile world, while others had been bred specifically for the Trials.

Some were intelligent, building traps and playing with their prey. Others were monsters full of claws, fangs, poisonous stingers; the stuff of nightmares. All of them had one thing in common: they killed for sport. I doubted they were aware of the role they played to entertain the intergalactic masses, but they played it well.

I had no idea what kind of beast I was tracking. The paw prints were large and deep, making me think of something much taller than me, but I couldn't see any claw marks at the edges of the paw prints. It didn't mean anything, though, since their claws might be retractable like my own. Four paws with six toes each.

The scent was off-putting, bitter and strangely nauseating. My instincts were telling me to run rather than walk towards the danger, but I kept going. It couldn't be much further. The beast had passed here only ten minutes or so ago. Now that I had a strong scent to follow and no longer had to rely on tracks on the ground, I was catching up quickly.

A peculiar rock caught my eye, glinting silver in the undergrowth. I picked it up only to realise it wasn't a rock at all. Metal crumpled into a ball by immense force. A drone camera, maybe. I'd not seen any cameras yet, but I knew they had to be out there. The reason they'd dropped me on the planet was so I could die for their entertainment, and they'd want to capture that. Depending on what kind of tech they used, cameras could be smaller than an orc's eye could see. Yet this lump of metal was the size of my fist.

I wasn't strong enough to turn metal into a round ball. What had done this? Was it the work of the predator I was tracking? Ancestors, I sure hoped not. That would end up a short fight resulting in my death before I could distract the game makers from my mate.

I let it fall to the ground, an unsolved riddle I didn't have time for, and continued my hunt. When the scent got so strong that it burned in my eyes, I pulled the axe from my kilt-belt. It was smaller than what I was used to fighting with and not well-balanced, but it was better than relying simply on my claws. They were diamond-coated, making them almost unbreakable, but fighting with my claws alone required me to get dangerously close to my enemy. Using the axe meant keeping some distance between us.

A strange chirping sound made me freeze. It had been quiet in the forest until now, not even a single bird singing in the canopy above. The rustling of leaves in the slight breeze had been the only sound. I doubted it was the predator, it reminded me too much of a cry for help.

Prey.

And the scent was leading me in the same direction as the sound was coming from. I didn't have time to help anyone but my mate, but this meant I might be able to hit two cli'ggres with one stone.

I continued walking, hastening my steps until I broke into a jog. I no longer tried to hide my presence. I pulled the image of my mate to the surface of my mind. Mating rage filled me and I used that fury to give me a boost of energy. My diamond-tipped claws extended from their sheaths, ready for battle.

The chirping echoed through the jungle again, a desperate sound that made me increase my pace. I was running now, battle rage taking over.

As I broke through a patch of thick undergrowth, a horrific scene presented itself. Two rakefangs, their claws dripping with blood, spittle flying from their gaping maws, had cornered a tiny animal. It was laying on its side, deep gashes marring its golden fur. No, not fur. Feathers. It had curled up into a ball, covering its head with its paws, but that would offer no protection against the rakefangs.

I'd seen them tear apart contestants, not because they were hungry but because they enjoyed causing pain. They were huge beasts with six legs, sleek fur as black as the night, and cruel yellow eyes. They got their name from the terrifying fangs protruding from their jaws, sharp and poisonous. Once scratched by the fangs, their victims would be drained of energy. Not paralysed, that would be no fun to the monsters, but weakened enough to not present much of a challenge.

Rakefangs were among the worst predators on Kalumbu. I may have thought I'd be able to handle one, with enough preparation and my own weapons, but now I was facing two of them with neither the weapons I favoured nor the energy and strength I'd need to fight them.

Sensing my presence, the rakefangs turned from their injured prey, fixing their cruel gaze on me. They had four lidless eyes above scar-covered nostrils, each more menacing than the next.

"How about you play with someone more of a challenge?" I shouted. I had to draw the cameras' attention. Were there any drones nearby? Were they watching me just now? I had to chance it.

"I will kill you," I growled, raising my axe dramatically. "You shouldn't have got in my way."

The rakefangs exchanged a glance that told of more intelligence than I'd expected, then lifted their fleshy lips, snarling wildly. Their fangs were glistening with poison and blood. I'd have to stay clear of them. Keep them at a distance, strike quickly before retreating. That was the only strategy that would work here. Despite my battle experience, I knew I was outmatched. The rakefangs were bred to be killers, ruthless and effective.

I could only hope that I could draw out the fight, catch the game makers' attention and distract them from my mate for long enough to buy her some time.

Behind the rakefangs, the wounded animal lifted its small head to find out why the attack had stopped. It had three eyes that seemed too big for its head, framed by tiny golden feathers. Its gaze met mine, just for a moment, but something *shifted* within me. I had no words for the sensation. It was as if a wall that I hadn't even realised existed crumbled deep inside me, releasing a flood of power. Fresh, cooling energy streamed through my body, rejuvenating me. My vision became sharper, my stance steadier. Suddenly, I felt as if I'd never been starved, imprisoned and deprived of sleep. I was at the top of my game, a predator in my own right, and I could take on these beasts.

The rakefangs snarled again, then they attacked. They flew through the air, claws extended, fangs ready to dig deep into my flesh, but I was ready. I jumped to the left, causing one of them to crash against the tree behind me. My axe was ready for the other. The blade nicked the beast's throat, but it was faster than I had anticipated and evaded most of my blow. Hot black blood sprayed all over me, burning on my skin, but the rakefang didn't even seem to notice the injury.

The other growled from behind me, announcing its deadly intentions.

I tightened my grip on the axe and sent a prayer to my ancestors.

7

FAY

I was being pulled into all directions, invisible forces tearing me apart. I screamed as pain unlike anything I'd ever felt assaulted my body. The scream was swallowed by the mist surrounding me. Just when I thought I'd pass out from the pain and the pulling, the tension lessened and reversed. The pull became a push. A different kind of pain, no less intense. Instead of being torn apart, I was now crushed, squeezed into a mould I didn't fit into. My throat was hoarse from the soundless screams that I couldn't repress. Agony was all I was. Pain was my existence. Had there been a life before the suffering?

I didn't know how long it lasted. It could have been days. When the pressure finally abated, I was a mess of tangled limbs. I found myself lying on soft ground, my cheeks wet with tears, a minty scent all around me. I slowly opened my eyes. I'd not even realised that they'd been squeezed shut.

Large golden leaves, as long as my arm, covered the ground. Above me, the canopy was the same colour, trees once again hiding the sky. Instead of purple, these had yellow bark, a deep sunflower yellow interspersed by shining flecks of gold. Had the sun been able to pierce the thick cover of leaves, I was sure the tree trunks would have sparkled in its light.

Slowly, I sat up. Nausea lured in wait, threatening to rise up my throat, so I kept my movements slow and gentle. Whatever had happened had almost killed me. The pain had stopped, but I felt weak and spent.

Something warm wrapped around my wrist.

Chirp, chirp.

I wasn't surprised to see Chirpy by my side, one tail curled around my wrist, the other tapping impatiently on the ground. It chittered happily, clearly not aware that I'd just experienced the worst pain in my entire life.

Chirp, chirp, purr.

"What are you trying to tell me?" I asked before clearing my throat. My voice was raspy and didn't quite sound like myself.

Chirrrrrrrrp.

The little animal climbed up my arm and settled back on my shoulder, never stopping its happy chirping. One tail once again wrapped around my neck, the other around my upper arm.

I staggered to my feet to take in my new surroundings. I'd travelled into an entirely different area. It could have been a different planet for all I knew. Teleportation? Beaming? Whatever had happened, I didn't want to do it ever again. My body still didn't feel quite right, like it had been put together the wrong way.

The colours around me matched those of little Chirp. Everything was painted in golden, brown and ochre hues. No more bright colours like before. It almost looked as if the forest was drenched in sunlight, but a quick look up told me that no sunrays were able to pierce the canopy. The ground was hidden beneath massive leaves but I bet the earth was golden as well. The trees surrounding us were just as huge as the ones by the lake, but the bark was different, shinier and smoother. Thick roots curled around their trunks like a snake before digging deep into the ground. The roots weren't as smooth as the rest of the tree, instead they were covered in tiny sharp thorns. I'd have to watch where I stepped here; I really didn't want to tear open the soles of my feet even more.

Chirp, chirp.

My companion pointed to the right. Once again, I let it guide me through the forest. I walked slowly, both to make sure I didn't step on any thorny roots and because I felt absolutely shattered. I hoped Chirpy was leading me to somewhere I could rest. Not that I'd fit into its burrow, hole, nest or whatever else it has as its home.

After maybe fifteen minutes of following Chirpy's directions, a path began to appear, well-trodden. Leaves had been brushed to the side, revealing the sandy ground for the first time. And yes, it was golden, almost like wet sand on a beach but more sparkly. I was starting to miss seeing other colours than just hues of yellow and brown.

Walking on the path was easier and I increased my pace a little, no longer having to worry about those painful-looking roots. I was wondering who'd created the path. Animals or other beings? Predators or prey?

Chirpy stopped chattering and only chirped whenever I had to change direction slightly. There were no other sounds in the forest. No birds, no animal cries, barely even the rustle of leaves. It was eerily quiet. The calm before the storm?

At some point, the sound of flowing water broke the silence. We got to a stream that cut through the path, only a foot wide, with bright red water that looked entirely unnatural. Chirpy jumped off me, landing with an elegant ninja roll. Using a fallen branch to anchor itself, it leant forward and drank greedily. If the water was safe for Chirpy, did that mean it was safe for me as well? It didn't look drinkable, not with that red colour that made me think something was bleeding into the water upstream. But I was thirsty.

I dipped one finger into the stream and cautiously tasted the water. It had a slight metallic note to it - not helping with the thought of it being mixed with blood that just wouldn't get out of my mind. I watched Chirpy drink its fill for a while, trying to make up my mind. I could continue on and hope to find another source of water that seemed less suspect, but what was the guarantee that there was any non-bloody water in this forest? This might be the only stream in the area. I needed to regain my strength and I couldn't do that without water.

Decision made, I cupped my hands and immersed them in the cold water. My skin tingled slightly. Squeezing my eyes shut so I wouldn't have to see the ominous colour, I drank. The metallic taste was strong and after I'd drunk, I felt like my tongue and cheeks were covered in an alien substance. Yuck.

Chirpy returned to its place on my shoulder and pointed one tail across the stream where the path continued. I took another sip while craving fresh water to wash that disgusting taste from my mouth.

Chirp, chirp.

The little animal sounded impatient.

"Alright, let's continue. I hope you know where you're leading me. And I very much hope that there will be shelter and food. Is it too late to warn you that I don't want to be eaten by your extended family?"

Chirpy made a choked sort of chirp, as if it was laughing at me.

"Yeah, you go and laugh. You're not stranded on an alien planet with a two-tailed monkey as my only guide. Although if our roles were reversed, you'd probably be in a lab by now, prodded by scientists. Maybe this is better. At least I'm free to explore this place. Whatever and wherever it is."

I rambled on, filling the silence. Chirpy responded with its cutesy sounds.

After another twenty minutes of walking or so, we

came to the biggest tree I'd seen so far. The trunk was as wide as a house and it was so tall that I couldn't see how far up it reached. Branches by surrounding trees seemed to join with the mammoth tree's trunk, forming a natural roof. And at the bottom of the tree, where the others had roots wrapped around, this one had an opening. Darkness lurked beneath the triangular gap that was almost tall enough for me to walk through.

Chirpy chittered and pointed both tails at the entrance in impatience. It clearly wanted me to go into the tree.

"Not the weirdest thing I've done today," I muttered just when an ear-splitting roar echoed through the forest. The sound made me want to cower and hide, hoping that whatever predator had roared would pass me by and eat something else. A wave of shivers ran down my back.

The alien monkey wrapped both tails around my neck and patted my ear with its paws while squeaking softly. I guessed that was Chirpy-language for "go and hide, you stupid, slow human".

Suddenly, the dark tree-cave no longer seemed as threatening. It actually felt welcoming; a safe place to hide from the monsters in the forest. I ducked my head and walked into the tree.

8
VRUHAG

My claws were sore and dripping with blood. I wavered, exhaustion catching up with me, but one rakefang was still alive and I couldn't rest just yet. The other lay dead on the ground, surrounded by its own innards. The cost of bringing down the beast had been high. Deep gashes on my upper arms and chest oozed blood. The remaining rakefang had bitten my ankle and it hurt to put weight on that foot. I could feel its poison spreading through my body, but it didn't hinder me as much as I'd expected. I still had some strength left in me, not completely drained of energy as I'd seen other Trials contestants after an encounter with a rakefang.

My axe was gone, probably beneath the monster's corpse, but it didn't matter. I was so filled with battle rage that my claws had become my favoured weapon.

The rakefang circled me, limping slightly but still a formidable threat. One of its eyes was gone. I didn't even remember how that happened. Everything had been a whirl of claws and fangs and pain. Only the thought of my mate was keeping me on my feet. I couldn't give up, not while there was still a chance that she was out there, alive. I'd know if she was dead. I was certain of it. I'd go mad, the mating fever accelerating into its final stage where I'd lose all sense of self. I'd seen males in the grips of the last phase. It was the worst thing that could happen to an orc. They'd had to be put down, killed by their friends and family before they could harm those they loved.

The little golden animal chirped weakly, as if to encourage me. It was still in the same place as before, too wounded to move, but it was watching the battle with surprising intelligence. Its three eyes were wide open and its gaze fixed on me. At least there would be someone to witness my death, if this fight ended in defeat. It made me feel better. I wasn't going to be completely alone in my last moments.

A snarl was my only warning, then the rakefang attacked once more. It could no longer jump as high as before, but it was still ferocious. Claws extended, fangs glistening with poison, cruel fury in its lidless eyes. I tumbled backwards, escaping most of its claws, but I'd miscalculated and the beast landed on top of me rather than fly further. The wind was knocked out of me as four heavy paws pushed down on my chest. Its front legs had landed on the ground, but its lower half had me pinned down. Old scars crisscrossed its chest and belly, along with a festering wound that ran all the way from its ribcage to its crotch. The wound was clearly infected with pus oozing from several places. Without thinking, I made a fist and punched as hard as I could.

The rakefang howled in pain as the wound reopened. Pus and blood rained down on me. A rotten smell filled the air, causing bile to rise in my throat. I fought against the instinct to vomit at both the sight and the smell.

The beast's legs quivered, giving me the chance to push it to one side. It staggered as if drunk. I rolled to the opposite side and jumped back to my feet. A sharp pain reminded me of my injured ankle, but there was no time to dwell on it. The rakefang was trying to regain its balance while yet more fluid dripped from its wound. I had to act while it was weakened. With my diamond-tipped claws fully extended, I threw myself at it from the side. My claws formed new gashes on the beast's sleek fur, but it moved faster than I'd thought possible, twisting around and clamping its jaws around my arm.

I screamed as sharp fangs dug deep into my flesh, spreading yet more poison. A coldness seeped through my body. I must not have got a full dose of poison from the ankle bite, but this time it was exactly like I'd feared. The cold turned into numbness, draining my energy. My knees buckled. I only had moments before I'd be too weak to fight. I only had one last chance.

I let my legs collapse under me, pretending to faint. The rakefang let go of my arm, which was exactly what I'd hoped for. As soon as I hit the ground, I punched upwards with all my strength, once again hitting the beast's wound. Flesh tore and with the most horrific squelching sound, a jellied mass dropped from its belly.

The rakefang howled a final time, then collapsed. It was still breathing, but the end was nigh.

Hate blazed in its eyes as it glared at me. It lifted one front paw as if to threaten me, but it was too weak to do anything else.

I wasn't faring much better. The poison had sapped me of all remnants of strength. I was on the ground, barely able to move. I'd heard that rakefang poison wasn't deadly, but if it kept me in this feeble state for long, I was as good as dead anyway. Every predator in the vicinity would have heard our fight, smelled the blood. They'd be coming soon to check for leftovers.

With one final snarl, the rakefang died. I watched as its cruel eyes turned milky and its body went still. A horrific end for a horrible creature.

A weak chirp caught my attention. The golden-feathered animal was behind me, but I was too weak to turn around.

"Sorry, I can't help you," I groaned. "I'm sorry if I merely delayed your death."

It chirped again. If it had any intelligence, it's language wasn't installed on my implant.

From the moment I'd first left my planet, I'd learned that size and appearance were no indicators of intelligence. Take the gloobs, for example, huge gelatinous blobs that were able to think faster than any other living being in the galaxy. Unfortunately, they also lacked the patience to share their wisdom with the rest of us.

For all I knew, this little animal was a sentient species. I'd never seen one of them in the Trials, but they weren't the kind of scary predators the game makers favoured. There was no reason for them to show any harmless fauna that bore no threat to contestants.

A shuffling noise behind me forced me to gather my last strength to turn around. My body felt heavier than it should. The little golden beast was dragging itself towards me, clawing at the ground to pull itself along. It clearly wasn't able to walk, but for some reason it felt it had to get closer to me. I wanted to reach out and help it, but I'd spent my last reserves. I couldn't even extend my arm.

Helpless, all I could do was watch, while always being aware that other predators might already be on the way. My senses were muddled and concentrating on my surroundings was difficult. I knew that if I closed my eyes, I'd drift off into unconsciousness. A death sentence. I had to stay awake and wait for the poison to leave my bloodstream. All I could do was hope that my body's fast metabolism would deal with it quickly.

When the little animal finally reached me, it was panting and trembling with exhaustion.

"Well done," I said, my words slurred. "Now what?"

In response, it slowly wrapped its two feathered

tails around my wrist. I would have pulled back if I'd had the energy. I didn't like being touched. Not that this animal seemed to care. It snuggled against my arm, chirping softly. I could feel its fast heartbeat when it pressed its chest to my skin. I had to admit it felt nice, like a miniature hug.

Orcs didn't *hug*. With our sires and friends, we might link arms if we felt particularly emotional. A mother might give her younglings a pat on the head. Embracing a fellow orc would result in battered balls and kicked-in teeth. But I'd watched aliens do it and always wondered what it would feel like.

Chirp, chirp, purr. The beastie looked pleased with itself. Its tails were still tightly wrapped around my wrist. It shuffled even closer until its snout was pressed against the inside of my arm. It looked up at me with three eyes that were too big for its face.

So cute.

It opened its mouth and before I could react, it rammed its sharp teeth into my arm.

9
FAY

I was in shock. Chirpy didn't seem to realise, introducing me to its extended family, while I could do nothing but gape and stare.

The interior of the tree was a palace, carved into the living wood with much detail and decoration. I stood in what could best be described as a courtyard. It was wide enough that I could have laid down comfortably without bumping against any of the walls and archways leading further into the tree. Tiny market stalls lined the edges of the courtyard, but the stalls were abandoned, with everyone gathering around me now. Beautifully carved columns grew all around the sides, supporting terraces arranged in circles that seemed to go on forever, up and up into the tree. I couldn't see the end of them. There had to be thousands of burrows on the terraces, each with a balcony giving a view of the courtyard. Warm sunlight came through gaps high above, amplified somehow. Mirrors, maybe? The golden light reflected on Chirpy's fur, making it seem like it was on fire. Stunning. Yet nobody looked at the alien monkey.

I was the star attraction. Hundreds, no, thousands of Chirpy-lookalikes stared down at me. Their combined chitter was so loud it was almost painful. They clearly were as fascinated by me was I was by them.

The longer I looked at the crowd of spectators, the more I began to notice the differences. Some of Chirpy's relatives had only one tail, others three. Their feathers weren't all the same shiny golden hue, some were brown and yellow shades. A few of them had a crown of feathers sprouting from their forehead, giving them a slightly rebellious air. Chirpy-punks.

My little companion climbed me like a tree and settled on my shoulder. It chirped, clearly wanting attention, but nobody was listening. With a frustrated chitter, Chirpy inflated its cheeks, then let out the air with a loud bellow.

Finally, the crowd fell silent, although a few in the higher terraces still chirped quietly. Chirpy began to talk while gesticulating with its tails. At least that's what I interpreted it as. It repeatedly pointed at my wrist until I raised my arm, showing the golden mark. Chirpy gave me an approving pat on the ear and continued its speech.

I wished I could understand what it was saying. I'd clearly underestimated its intelligence. This group of feathered monkeys had language, a society and had even carved their own homes. They were sentient. I felt like apologising to Chirpy for thinking about it as an animal. It was so much more.

When Chirpy finished, the chatter began anew as its relatives discussed whatever they'd just heard. Chirpy squeezed the top of my ear. Was it to reassure me or itself?

A blasting sound, akin to a trumpet being blown, filled the inside of the tree and the alien monkeys fell silent. Chirpy's tails tightened around my neck and arm. It was worried.

Unless I was completely misinterpreting the situation and it was getting ready to strangle me so that I could become an all-you-can-eat-buffet for its family.

No, I doubted I was in danger from these adorable beings. They didn't vibe threatening, just curious. And Chirpy itself had been nothing but helpful so far. I just wished I could understand what they were saying.

The trumpet stopped, making the silence that followed feel heavy and ominous. Footsteps echoed through the quiet tree, along with a dragging sound. Chirpy squeaked quietly and tightened its grip on me even more. Its tail around my throat was almost too tight, but I didn't want to draw attention to me by asking it to move a little.

From the opposite end of the tree hall, a dark shadow approached. It was much taller than Chirpy and its mates, likely reaching all the way up to my navel if it stood next to me. That explained why everything in here was oversized for Chirpy.

The alien stepped into the light. It looked similar to Chirpy and the others, except that it had four tails that were all erect behind its feathered body. It was mostly gold but there were silver spots along its shoulders and chest, glittering impressively. Its three eyes were a deep bronze and when its gaze met mine, a shiver ran down my back. Not fear, no. Respect. Awe. Some primal urge to bow and submit to this being came over me. I didn't resist. I inclined my head, breaking eye contact.

The giant monkey - well, on Earth it would have been the size of a chimpanzee, but compared to Chirpy it was huge - stepped towards me, two tails now pointing at me. My wrist itched and when I lifted my arm, I realised the golden mark was glowing brightly. What the fuck?

As if in a trance, I suddenly knew exactly what to do. I dropped to my knees, my arm extended. Chirpy jumped off my shoulder and stood by my side, one paw on my hip for reassurance. The four-tailed monkey approached me until my fingers almost touched its chest. Its gaze was fixed on me, the three bronze eyes unblinking and filled with emotions I couldn't interpret. One of its tails wrapped around my wrist and pulled my arm down. A second tail joined the first and as soon as they covered the golden mark, a bright light flashed before my inner eye and the world around me disappeared.

There was only me, the four-tailed monkey and white light all around us. Even Chirpy was no longer by my side.

"Can you understand me?" the being asked in a warm, feminine voice.

"I can. How is this happening? No, *what* is happening?"

"My great-great-grand-pup started the mind-link with you, but she wasn't strong enough to complete the bond. She's still young and you are her first. Now that I have fixed the link, you will be able to talk to her like you are talking to me. I am Ta'quii, clan-mother to my people. Tell me, what are you? I have not seen one of your kind before, yet you clearly are not dissimilar from us. Even though you lack a tail."

"I'm human. From Earth, or at least that's what we call my planet. I'm not sure how I got here or why I was taken. I woke up in a strange room, then they removed my clothes, there were lots of lights and noise, and then I somehow ended up in a lake."

I realised how crazy that story sounded. Especially when told to a four-tailed monkey who looked like they were coming from an acid-induced hallucination.

"Where am I?" I asked.

"That question has many answers," the being said with a slight laugh. "For us, it's home. For the invaders, it's an arena to play their twisted games in. It sounds like you have unwittingly become part of those games."

"Games? How can I be in a game without knowing?"

"Life is a game, the greatest of them all. We play to survive. The invaders have taken that idea and twisted it. They drop strangers like you on our world, then watch them try to survive. Most don't. We have learned to stay hidden, away from both those who play the game and those who organise it. Most have twisted souls and would only mean us harm. You, however, have a pure heart. Ali'quii recognised that. It's why she began the mind-link with you."

Ali'quii. That had to be Chirpy.

"What happens now?" I asked when the being didn't continue. "Is there a way for me to get home?"

"We do not have the means to transport you from our world. However, it is not time for you to leave yet. The trees tell me of someone searching for you. He has stumbled through our lands, unseeing, but now Ali'quii's Chosen has mind-linked with him. They are on their way here now. Until he arrives, we have much to talk about."

I only understood half of what I was being told. Someone searching for me? How was that possible? No one knew I'd been abducted from Earth. And even if someone had witnessed my alien abduction, they didn't have the means to travel through space to bring me home.

"Who is he?" I asked. "Is he human?"

"He is your mate."

10
VRUHAG

I couldn't stop staring at the golden rings around my wrist. They were bright against my green skin, reminding me of the permanent war paint of my ancestors. Right next to the golden markings were the bite marks, four tiny puncture wounds that had only bled one drop of blood each.

The little beastie had licked up the blood before I could stop it, and hadn't stopped chittering happily since. I left it to its chirping and let my attention drift to our surroundings. I was still too weak to move, so knowing that predators were approaching wouldn't help. Luckily, I couldn't pick up on any threatening scents or sounds. For now, we were safe.

The tips of my fingers tingled. Was that a sign that the poison was disappearing from my blood stream? Or was it a symptom of something bad?

I hated being this powerless. All I could do was lie

on the forest ground and wait for the poison to be vanquished.

Chirp, chirp, chitter, working? It should be working by now.

A voice, high-pitched but male, rang through my mind at the same time as my ears were picking up the beastie's chittering noises.

Maybe I should bite him again.

Were auditory hallucinations a symptom of rake-fang poisoning? I couldn't remember seeing that on the Trials, but I'd only watched a few episodes and that was a long time ago.

Yes, I will bite. Harder this time. Drink more blood. It was quite tasty.

"You will do no such thing," I roared, or at least I tried. I didn't have the energy. It came out as barely a whisper. A wave of shame washed over me. If my mate saw me like this, she'd run, tearing up the mating bond. Who'd want to be mated to a weakling like me? I wouldn't stay weak, but the fact that I was in this situation now was telling. Maybe I wasn't the strong warrior I'd imagined.

Wait, I'd understood the beastie. Heard it speaking in my head. Impossible.

You're not very clever, are you?

"You're talking to me," I muttered, dumbfounded. "How can I suddenly understand you? My translator implant shouldn't be able to get updates on Kalumbu. The planet is shielded."

Definitely not clever. Great. I mind-linked to an

idiot. Biting is still an option. It might make him more intelligent.

"No biting," I huffed. "Explain it then, little know-it-all. How are we talking?"

You don't listen, either. This isn't going to work.

"I listen-" I protested, before going over what the beastie had said. Mind-linked to an idiot. Linked.

"What kind of link?" I asked.

Total idiot. Didn't I say mind-linked? Yes, I did. How can you misunderstand that? Mind. Linked. Your mind linked to mine. Urgh, my Chosen will look down on me for linking to such a halfwit."

"Your Chosen, is that like your mate?"

Obviously. She mind-linked with someone much more intelligent. Good for her. Why do I always have to be the one with bad luck? First I get attacked by rakefangs, then I end up mind-linked to an imbecile. What's next?

"Stop insulting me," I growled. "I am Vruhag, a respected warrior. I saved your life. I will have you give me the respect I'm due."

The beastie looked up at me, annoyance flashing in its huge eyes. *I am Ano'quoo, second warrior priest to Ta'quii, the great clan mother. And I had the situation under control. No saving required. I would have vanquished the rakefangs if you hadn't distracted me.*

"Vanquished," I repeated, trying to discern whether the little creature was serious.

I was biding my time. Just because I'm not an overgrown giant like you doesn't mean I'm not a warrior.

Ano'quoo flashed his teeth at me, as if to remind me that he'd easily managed to bite me. I'd not put up any resistance. To be fair, I'd been way too surprised to react, and the poison in my bloodstream didn't help.

"Do you live on this planet?" I asked. "What is your species called?"

We are the Chii, children of Kalumbu. I don't need to ask what you are. Huge, smelly, dumb. An orc from Orcadia. I've seen your kind die. The others were braver than you. They didn't lie on the ground. Lazy.

I was tempted to show the beastie just how dangerous I could be. Lazy. I scoffed. As soon as the poison was metabolised, I'd challenge him to a fight. Then we'd know who the stronger of us was.

"Are there other orcs still alive here?"

For a moment, sadness seemed to pool in Ano'quoo's three eyes, then he chirped with irritation. *Of course not. Strangers arrive on Kalumbu, strangers die on Kalumbu. I shouldn't have bothered mind-linking to you. It won't be long until you join them in death.*

A growl rose in my throat. "Is that a threat?"

It's reality. The Chii have witnessed many deaths. We stay hidden, mourn from afar, pray for the souls. Nobody survives for long without help.

"I will survive," I said with renewed strength. "I have to find my mate. She was dropped somewhere on this planet and I won't stop until she's safe. So I swear."

Ano'quoo curled one tail around the golden mark on my wrist. *She's already safe. My Chosen is looking after her. Once you stop being lazy, we can go and see them.*

"I'm not lazy... Wait, you know my mate?"

I can see her through my Chosen's mind-eye. She is not an orc.

"I know. And it doesn't matter." I tried to sit up, but my vision blurred at the effort. The poison was still too strong.

What is she? She's very naked. No fur, no feathers. Not even a tail. Are you sure she's your mate?

I flashed my fangs at him. If I'd been at my full strength, I would have wrapped my hand around his neck. "She's my mate and she's perfect."

If you say so. She's nowhere near as pretty as my Chosen. Just wait until you meet Ali'quii. She's not only the prettiest female in our clan, she's also the great-great-granddaughter of the clan mother herself. She's from a powerful lineage. Our pups will be stunning.

Ano'quoo smiled dreamily before turning his stern gaze at me once more. *How long until you can walk?*

"I'm not sure. It's not like I've ever been bitten by a rakefang before. And-"

A crack in the undergrowth made me freeze. Ano'quoo had heard it as well. His feathers puffed up as he made himself look bigger, a defence mechanism that didn't really work. He still didn't appear threatening in the least, on the contrary, he now resembled a fluffy ball. Any youngling would have loved to play with him.

We need to go. Now.

He was right, but I didn't see how it could work. I was barely strong enough to lift my head. Walking seemed out of the question.

I will bite you to give you more antivenom. But I will be weak after. You will have to carry me.

He sounded extremely disgruntled about that. I supposed he was a proud male, no matter his size. I respected him for it.

"I will defend you until you recover," I promised solemnly. "What direction is my mate?"

I will guide you. Prepare for pain.

I was about to tell him that I was a warrior, that I didn't fear pain, but he'd already wrapped his tiny claws around my wrist, his fangs ready to strike.

Time slowed down as his teeth descended towards my skin. I forced myself to stay still when his fangs dug into my flesh, more painful than I thought possible. All my instincts were screaming at me to destroy him, to turn him into a stuffed animal for my future younglings. But I didn't move, letting him inject me with the antivenom. Icy cold flowed through my veins, before my blood seemed to boil. I grit my teeth, my tusks digging into my upper lip. Sweat pooled on my skin, evaporating immediately while I suffered the worst fever I'd ever experienced.

It was over as quickly as it had started. I jumped to my feet, surprised how fast my strength had returned. The movement in the undergrowth was becoming louder. Whatever was making its way towards us would arrive any moment now. It was time to leave.

I scooped up Ano'quoo and sat him on my shoulder. He weakly clung on, his eyes droopy and without the earlier sparkle.

North, he whispered in my head.

I turned in that direction and started to run as fast as I could.

11

FAY

A chii male handed me a wooden mug the size of a thimble. Steam rose from the lime-green liquid inside.

"Tea?" I asked Ali'quii. My little friend was perched on my shoulder, proudly staring at the crowd surrounding us. I was the star attraction and more chii kept arriving to take a look at me.

Yes, whitebark tea, she said in my head. It would take some time getting used to hearing her in my mind. I felt like apologising for thinking she was just an animal. Now that I could communicate with her, I realised I couldn't have been more wrong.

I emptied the mug in one sip. The hot liquid burned down my throat, leaving a minty taste in my mouth. Not bad. Another chii, this one with only one tail, immediately took my empty mug and replaced it with a full one. I'd have to do this about twenty times if I wanted a human-sized cup of tea. Someone should have told me that this planet was a bring-your-own-mug establishment.

Do you like it? Ali'quii asked. Her mental voice was sweet and melodic. There was a definite family resemblance to Ta'quii, although the clan mother had sounded a lot older.

I had so many questions for Ali'quii. About her, about her people, about the planet. And about the mate Ta'quii had mentioned. She'd refused to answer any further questions about him, saying that it wouldn't take long until he'd get here.

Two hours had passed, two hours of being stared at by thousands of chii. Their excited chirping echoed through the hollow tree; a cacophony of sound. I was only able to understand Ali'quii and Ta'quii. When they spoke to me, I heard their chittering with my ears but understood their meaning with my mind. It was a strange way of communicating. I'd not dared to ask if they could understand all my thoughts, or only if I consciously directed them at the chii.

A feathered paw nudged my hand and I released my empty mug. A new one was handed to me, this time containing a ruby red liquid.

"Yes, I like it," I said, realising I'd never answered Ali'quii's question. "What's this one?"

Warberry juice. It's my favourite.

The juice was tangy with a tart aftertaste. Just when I thought I wouldn't want another cup of this, even the size of a thimble, a burst of syrupy sweetness exploded on my tongue. Shortly after, a pleasant warmth throbbed in my throat.

Ali'quii was looking at me expectantly, awaiting my verdict.

"That was different. I think I'll need another mug to appreciate it."

Chirpy barked an order and a second cup of warberry juice was pushed into my hand. This time, I swirled the juice in my mouth, waiting for the sweetness to arrive, but it stayed tart and unpleasant. What a strange drink that only revealed its hidden taste after swallowing.

They served me five other drinks, each more colourful and surprising than the next, but in the end, I asked for more whitebark tea. A chii female arrived with a tray as big herself, laden with at least thirty tiny mugs full of the green liquid. That would keep me going for a while.

"Please tell them thank you," I asked Ali'quii.

She chirped something at the four chii who'd served my drinks. They puffed up their chests, turning into golden feather balls. So cute. I resisted the temptation to pick them up and cuddle them. I doubted that would go down well.

"Do you live here?"

Yes, on the thirty-seventh floor. I would show you, but I doubt you'd fit up the stairs. Mirth echoed in her mental voice. *We have not had such a big visitor in a long time. The clan mother says that once, we had guest quarters for non-chii, but that was before...*

"Before what?" I asked when she didn't continue.

Before they turned our home into an arena. Before they sent warriors down here to die.

"How long has it been like this?"

She gave the mental equivalent of a shrug. *All my life. All my parents' lives. Ta'quii is the only one who remembers. There used to be big two-leggers, not unlike you. Their ruined buildings remain, but the beings disappeared long ago, killed by the same invaders who now send the death-bound warriors. We used one of their portals earlier. Only a few of them are still active, run by some magic we don't understand. My Chosen will take a portal to get here. I can feel him. He's getting closer.*

"Explain it to me, about the Chosen. Is that like your husband?"

I don't know that word. Husband. My Chosen is my mate, chosen for me by the ancestors. They have watched me all my life, protecting me, guiding me, and now they have found the perfect mate for me. He is not of our tribe, so I've not met him before, but as soon as the ancestors blessed us with the knowledge of our bond, he began his journey here.

She sounded excited at the prospect, but I couldn't help but wonder whether this was an arranged marriage where Ali'quii had no control.

"But what if you don't like him?" I asked carefully. "If you've never met him before, how can you be sure you'll be happy with him?"

Ali'quii smiled at me, her three eyes glowing with

confidence. *The ancestors know. There has never been a Chosen pair who didn't match perfectly. It's why it can take a long time to find one's Chosen. The ancestors never tell you until they're absolutely sure. They don't make mistakes.*

There was no trace of doubt in her mental voice. I envied her for that faith. I'd never had anything I believed in that blindly. As a journalist, I was used to questioning everything. Sometimes, I wished I could just stop doubting and find something to have faith in. Or someone.

I don't think it's a coincidence, Ali'quii said and gently wrapped one tail around my neck.

"What is?"

That I found you and my Chosen found your mate. The ancestors were guiding us. I've never heard of them taking an interest in non-chii, but maybe you're special. Maybe...

Her eyes went wide as she stared at me as if she was seeing me for the first time. Her claws dug into my shoulder.

"What?" I asked.

I have to talk to the clan mother.

She hopped off my shoulder and disappeared into the crowd. Some of the gathered chii gave her curious looks, but their attention quickly returned to me. I smiled at them, feeling entirely out of place. I'd travelled the world, seen many exotic places, but I'd never felt so alien as I did here. And that's what I was. An *alien*. To them, I was the alien from a faraway planet.

My head spun. Would I ever see my home again? Or would I spend the rest of my life surrounded by chii, trying to survive on a planet controlled by malevolent aliens?

I shuddered at the thought. As friendly and welcoming the chii were, they were not human. Not even humanoid. I couldn't talk to them. I doubt I could learn their chirping language. Ali'quii and Ta'quii would be my only way to communicate with the rest of the chii, but Ta'quii was the clan mother and probably terribly busy, and Ali'quii had her Chosen. Once he arrived, he'd be the focus of her attention.

I didn't even know where I'd sleep tonight. The centre of the hollow tree, where I was sitting just now, had enough space for me to stretch out, but this was also the chii's market and gathering place. I'd just get in the way. Their home wasn't made for humans.

An icy loneliness gripped my heart. I was surrounded by friendly creatures, yet I was alone nonetheless. Maybe the man travelling here this very moment was human. Mate. What a strange word, not one I'd ever used. It tasted of depravity, base needs and trashy romance novels. I preferred the chii's Chosen terminology. Chosen by the ancestors. Not that I wanted anyone, ancestor or not, choose my partner for me. Back home, I'd once written an article on arranged marriages in contemporary India. One of the women I'd interviewed, Pawan, had been fully supportive of the concept. Her parents knew her best, she'd argued, and therefore they were best placed to choose her husband. I'd almost envied her trust in her parents, just like I admired Ali'quii's faith in her ancestor's infallible wisdom. But I'd also spoken to many women who'd suffered as a result of the arranged marriage. Who'd ended up with violent men. Who'd been trapped in a loveless relationship.

No, it wasn't for me. I wanted to choose my own partner. Forge my own destiny. And if I chose wrong, I only had myself to blame. Or, most likely, I'd stay single for the rest of my probably very short life.

A movement in the crowd before me drew my attention. A deafening chitter erupted as hundreds of chii began to chirp excitedly. They all turned towards the main entrance, so I did the same, watching and waiting.

My Chosen has arrived, Ali'quii called in my mind. I looked around for her, but couldn't spot her in the chaotic crowd. At what distance were we able to communicate mentally? I added it to my ever growing list of questions. *And your mate is outside. He's too big to come in.*

There it was again, that word. Mate. Ali'quii simply accepted that some stranger was my...mate. I didn't. I'd have a look at him because I was curious and because I wanted to stretch my legs, but that was it. No commitment. No mate.

I scrambled to my feet, very careful not to step onto one of the gathered chii. They looked up at me, distracted for a moment, before turning their attention back to the entrance. Someone grabbed my leg. Ali'quii grinned up at me, her three eyes sparkling with excitement. She climbed me like a tree, settling on my shoulder.

Let's meet them.

She sounded thrilled. Her tails wrapped around my neck again, a now familiar, almost comforting sensation.

Hurry.

I carefully walked to the opening, only now noticing the slight shimmer in the air. A bit like the portal.

"What is that?" I asked Ali'quii. I should have talked to her in my head, but I'd forgotten all about that.

A shield. Did you think we'd leave our door open to predators?

The technology had to come from the ancient beings who'd become extinct since, just like the portals.

Ali'quii pressed one paw against my left ear, then howled like a tiny werewolf. Even with her paw plugging my ear, it was still loud enough to hurt.

The shimmering glitter disappeared. Curious. They controlled the technology with sounds. Had it been built that way or had they found a new way to make use of it? I ignored my inner journalist and stepped out of the tree, ducking low at the lowest point.

It had darkened outside, the forest turning dim and gloomy. The sun was no longer high enough to even attempt to pierce the thick canopy. It would be night soon. My stomach growled at the realisation that I'd been on this planet almost all day.

A huge shape rushed towards me, a tumble of claws and muscles and – were those tusks? He stopped right in front of me, so close that his scent, earth and sweat and something very, very masculine, assaulted my senses. He was huge, towering above me, his skin bright green, naked except for a kilt-like wrap around his hips. Barely healed wounds on his arms and chest spoke of past battles.

He stared at me with dark eyes, almost black. Hot breath hit my face. His gaze flicked up and down my body, then he looked past me, at the chii's home tree, his posture tense as if searching for a threat.

He said something in a deep, guttural voice. I didn't understand a word, but it sounded like a question. No, a demand.

He wants to know why you growled at him, Ali'quii translated.

This would be the perfect time to wake up from this crazy, ridiculous dream.

12
VRUHAG

My mate was even more beautiful in real life. Her auburn mane was redder than it had looked on screen, the knot she'd tied it in slowly dissolving, letting a few strands flow loose. They framed her pale face perfectly. Her mossy eyes were fixed on me, the intensity of her gaze speaking of an inner strength that her feeble body lacked. She was no longer naked, although the yellow moss wrapped around her middle didn't look like it would last for much longer. It only reached halfway down her thighs, while the upper edge didn't fully cover her breasts. I forced myself to look at her face. Her innocent, sweet face. No fangs, no tusks, just pale pink skin that looked too soft for this dangerous world.

Yet she'd growled at me. A sound I'd first mistaken for a predator before realising it had come from her. Did she not know I was her mate? Or was this part of her culture, a mating ritual maybe? Perhaps she'd challenged me to prove my prowess.

Idiot, come and pick me up!

Ano'quoo sounded furious. I looked at my empty arms, then dimly remembered dropping him as soon as I'd heard that growl. The mating fever had taken over, dispelling all rational thought. Ano'quoo had no longer mattered. Now that I stood opposite my mate, breathing in her sweet scent, bathing in her beauty, I couldn't get myself to feel guilty. She was the most important person in the universe. Everyone else could wait.

You brainless ogre! If you don't come right now, I will tell my Chosen to tell your mate that-

You can communicate with her? I interrupted. My mate hadn't understood when I'd asked her if she was alright. She'd not said anything yet, so I wasn't sure if my implant would be able to translate her language.

Pick. Me. Up. Now. I grimaced at his outraged mental yelling. My mate's eyes widened when she noticed my tusks. I presented them to her, proud of their size and width. It was said that the length of a male's tusks corresponded to the length of his... most important part. I didn't want to think of it. Didn't want to grow even harder. Ever since her scent had woken my mating fever back on the space station, I'd been semi-erect. Now, being in her presence, basking in that overpowering sweet scent of hers... It was hard to focus. Hard not to push her onto the forest ground and claim her as my mate.

I forced myself to turn around and walk away from

her. I didn't want her to see the monster. I had to control my primal urges in her presence. At least until we were alone. Then I'd claim her, ravish her, fuck her into oblivion. She'd scream my name and we'd become one, the stars our witness and-

An angry hiss prevented me from stepping on Ano'quoo. The little beastie was curled up on the ground, looking miserable. While I was back at full strength, giving me the antivenom had sapped all his remaining energy. Even after walking through the forest for hours, he still hadn't recovered.

I gently picked him up and cradled him on one arm, hoping he'd understand the wordless apology. Ano'quoo chittered angrily, but didn't speak to me in my mind. I carried him back to the enormous tree that my mate had stepped out of. It smelled like Ano'quoo, but a thousand times stronger. The den of his people, where his Chosen lived. No wonder he was so keen to be brought there. Although in his position, I'd be embarrassed to be carried by another male.

I hurried back to my mate. The chii female on her shoulder was a little larger than Ano'quoo, but the golden hue of her feathers was exactly the same. In contrast to her Chosen, the female's three eyes shone with warmth. I was glad my mate had met the kinder of the two chii. Ano'quoo was too rude and shouldn't be allowed in her presence.

As soon as I stopped in front of the two females, Ano'quoo chirped loudly. He made himself as big as

possible, his tails erect, his feathers fluffed up. Presenting himself to his Chosen. She'd see through the bluster soon enough.

I met my mate's gaze and her lips curled with amusement. I returned the smile.

"Can you understand me?" she asked, my implant translating perfectly. I hadn't expected her language to be programmed onto it, considering she came from a primitive planet, but it was a pleasant surprise.

"I can," I said, desperately hoping that they'd given her an implant before dropping her onto the planet.

"Wait, did you just answer my question because you understood or did you tell me that you can't understand what I'm saying? Her brow furrowed. "Nod if you can understand."

Obediently, I nodded, pleased that her species used the same gesture.

Her eyes lit up. "Great. You can understand me, but I can't understand you. I guess that was too much to hope for. At least the chii can translate for us."

But the two beasties were otherwise occupied. Their attention was focused on each other as they moved their tails in slow, precise movements; a dance of sorts. Their eyes were half-lidded, their expressions dreamy.

I exchanged another look with my mate.

"They're very cute," she muttered.

"They are," I agreed, before remembering that she couldn't understand me. I pressed one hand to my chest. "Vruhag."

She understood right away. "Fay."

I already knew that, but I much preferred the way she pronounced her name than the announcer had before she'd been dropped onto Kalumbu. Fay. My mate.

We stood in silence for a moment. I felt awkward and not just because of the translation issue. I also had a feathered beastie on my arm who was by now eye-fucking his mate. I felt like dropping him, but it may have interrupted whatever ritual they were conducting. Unless it wasn't a ritual and they really were fucking with their minds. I knew of at least two other species who preferred that to the physical act. Idiots, if you asked me, but after a day of running around with a hard shaft, I may have been biased.

"So, what are you?" my mate asked hesitantly. "Are you from this planet?"

I knew that she wouldn't understand my answer, but she'd already proven she was familiar with orc gestures. I nodded to answer her second question.

"Oh. I suppose you'll know if there's a way for me to get home?"

I wished she hadn't asked me that. I nodded sadly. She was trapped here, just like I was. We'd found each other, but we wouldn't have a long life together on Kalumbu. The game masters wouldn't let us settle down. They'd make sure we died as violently and dramatically as possible.

The cold truth of that made me clench my fists. I'd found my mate only to be destined to watch her die.

Ano'quoo's tails around my wrist tightened slightly. The feathered beastie didn't break eye contact with his Chosen, but it was clear he was still aware of what was happening around him. Namely, me about to smash something. I fought the anger at our hopeless situation, but I couldn't help but shake with suppressed fury and frustration.

"What's wrong?" my mate – Fay – asked. Her gaze flicked to my clenched fists before settling back on my face. I realised my mouth was open, tusks on full display; an offensive position. I forced myself back into a more relaxed pose and pressed my lips in a tight line.

"I'm almost glad you can't understand me, because this way I don't have to lie to you," I said. "But since you're my mate, I promise to always tell you the truth, no matter how unpleasant it may be. We were sent to this planet to die, all for the entertainment of others. They're filming this and are broadcasting it across the galaxy. I assume we have a moment of respite just now because they lost track of us when I travelled through the portals, but that won't last long. The cameras will be back. And if we aren't killed by predators, they'll send more contestants to finish us off. I am sorry, my mate. I will protect you until my last breath, but nobody has ever left Kalumbu alive."

I wanted to roar with anger, with helplessness, but it would only frighten her. So I stayed still, forcing a smile on my face, as if everything was alright. As if we weren't two dead mates walking.

"I will ask Ali'quii to translate that once she's...less distracted," Fay replied. "But I'm so glad you know how we can get away. Can you take me back to Earth? Do you have a spaceship?" She laughed; a beautiful sound that lightened the sorrow in my heart. "I never thought I'd ever ask that question. And I don't even know if you call them spaceships. Maybe they're called galaxy vessels or... Sorry, I ramble when I'm nervous."

She was adorable. Without thinking, I reached out and gently stroked her cheek. I had to know just how soft her skin really was. What her mane felt like when I curled it around my fingers. What her lips tasted like when-

She slapped my hand away. I stared at her in shock. She'd *slapped* me. Her mate. Then I grinned. There was fire in her veins. She was a suitable bride for an orc.

"Why are you smiling?" she snapped. "Forget it. I wouldn't understand the answer anyway."

Fay looked at her chii companion, then rolled her eyes. "Hurry up with whatever it is you're doing. I could use a translator."

The female chii didn't turn her attention away from her Chosen. They were still waving their tails, their gazes locked. For a moment, I wished this first encounter with *my* mate was as ritualistic as theirs. But there were no special orc rituals for the very first meeting. By the time most males found their mates, they were so deep within the mating fever that they claimed their females the second they lay eyes on them. I was lucky in that I'd found my mate within days of first smelling her scent. I still had full control over my actions, although now that I was close to her, so close her scent enveloped me like a cloud, it wouldn't be long until the base instincts in me took over.

I thanked the years of warrior training that had installed this discipline within me. I didn't want to frighten my soft little female by showing her the feral side of me right away.

The *soft little female* scowled at me. What she didn't have in physical prowess, she had in mental strength. She'd survived on Kalumbu for almost an entire day. Many great warriors had failed at that. Maybe there was more to her than met the eye.

"Since our little friends are too busy to translate, let's go back to basics. Nod for yes, shake your head for no. Got it?"

Nod for yes? Oh no. If that was her culture's meaning of the gesture, she'd have misunderstood my earlier replies. I tried to remember what I'd nodded to. Whether I was from this planet and whether I had a way to leave it. Klat. I'd given her hope where there was none.

I shouldn't have assumed that a nod meant no for her. Most species who carried their brains in their head had similar gestures, whether it was nodding, shaking the head or bobbing it from side to side, but the meaning wasn't always the same. In my excitement, I'd forgotten the prime rule of first contact: never assume; question everything.

Unaware of my inner turmoil, Fay asked her first question. "Do you know why I was brought here?"

Her, specifically? No, but I assumed she wanted to know the general purpose of our stay on Kalumbu: to die for sport.

I nodded.

"Alright, I'll ask you for more details later once our translators aren't busy eye-fucking. Were you involved in my abduction?"

I stared at her with wide eyes. How could she even ask that? Didn't she know that I was her mate? That I'd die to keep her safe? Couldn't she smell our bond?

I shook my head vehemently.

"Phew. That's good. I guess you could be lying, but I'm pretty good at spotting a lie." Her piercing gaze didn't make me doubt that for a single click. "Were you abducted as well?"

I almost shook my head, then remembered it was the other way round and nodded.

"I'm sorry," she said, her expression softening.

"Why are you sorry?" I asked. "It wasn't you who captured my ship, who put me in that cell. You had nothing to do with it. Why are you apologising on someone else's behalf?"

But of course she didn't understand me.

"I wish I knew what you're saying," Fay exclaimed, frustration lacing her melodic voice. A voice that I wanted to moan and scream my name. "I assume you don't speak English, so how do you understand me? Is it some kind of translating technology?"

I nodded and tapped the space behind my ears where the implants had been inserted.

Unfortunately, I forgot that Ano'quoo had still been perched on my arm. The chii hissed and buried its sharp claws in my flesh.

13

FAY

Watching the huge green man struggle with a furious golden chii was a rather comical sight. Ali'quii's Chosen chittered angrily while sinking its claws deep into Vruhag's arm. That had to hurt. Emerald green blood seeped from the scratches, a shade darker than his skin. I shouldn't have been surprised that alien blood wasn't red, but seeing it felt surreal. Funnily enough, it wasn't even the strangest aspect about the situation.

They are a good match for each other, Ali'quii said in my head. She sounded amused.

"Are you done saying hello to your Chosen?" I asked. I sounded a little annoyed, but I hoped she wouldn't notice. Seeing her so in sync with her mate while struggling to communicate with Vruhag had been frustrating.

We only just began, she said with a chuckle. *The welcoming ritual lasts for days. But we reached a good point to take a break. How are you getting on with your Chosen?*

"He can understand me but I can't understand him. Can you translate for us?"

She shot a pointed look at the two males, who were still fighting. Vruhag growled at the chii male, flashing his tusks. Besides his size, they were the most alien feature about him. Well, and the green skin, the fact he only had four fingers, and the pointed ears. He was humanoid, but no human man could be that *bulky*. He was layers and layers upon hard muscles; a predator born for battle. He was clearly holding back, not using his full strength as he tried to pry the chii off his arm. Thick drops of green blood splattered onto the forest ground, but Vruhag didn't even seem to notice.

Several thick scars marred his chest. Newer gashes, only just closed, covered his arms and torso. He'd seen worse fights before.

A roar in the distance made everyone freeze. Something was out there. For a moment, I'd forgotten that I was on a hostile planet where not everyone was as welcoming as the chii.

We should go inside, Ali'quii said.

"Will he fit?"

There's a cave below the tree. It'll be big enough for the two of you. Although you might have to snuggle close together if you want to lie down.

She sounded amused by the thought. I wasn't. I didn't want to *snuggle* with this stranger. I wanted him to take me home. I wanted to ignore how good he *smelled*. How attractive he looked despite the alienness. How I had the strange urge to get to know him. To curl up in his arms.

I pushed the thought away. All this talk of mates and Chosen was affecting me. I didn't need a mate. I needed a spaceship pilot.

"Lead the way," I told Ali'quii and shot a look at the males. They'd stopped fighting, although they were still glaring at each other. Blood was dripping down Vruhag's arm. The chii had done some real damage. I hoped Vruhag would heal more quickly than humans.

Ali'quii grasped my ear with her paw for support, her tails wrapping around my neck once again. She directed me around the tree, past the entrance, to where two roots rose from the ground, forming a half-circle. Moss and lichen hung from the roots, a natural curtain hiding whatever lay beyond.

Through there. Watch your step, it goes down quite steeply.

I pulled the plant curtain aside, revealing only darkness. Vruhag reached over me and took hold of the curtain, as if I couldn't do it myself. I glared at him. He looked confused by my reaction, but didn't let go of the lichen.

I cautiously walked into the darkness, every step taking me further into the unknown.

Mind your head, Ali'quii warned, and I ducked low. Vruhag would have to kneel if the passage was too low for me to stand up straight. The thought made me smile. He had the air of a man who wasn't used to kneeling in front of anyone.

The air was musky and cool, lacking the exotic scents of the jungle.

Stretch out your paws and rub the walls.

"They're called hands," I said, but did as Ali'quii had instructed. I touched something soft and strangely warm. Light flared around my hand and when I stepped back, my handprint now glowed on a layer of turquoise moss that seemed to cover the walls of the cave. Fascinated, I touched it again and again, leaving dozens of glowing handprints behind. Beautiful. It reminded me of ancient stone age cave paintings. How long would the glow last? It was just about sufficient light to let me estimate the dimensions of the cave. It was high enough for Vruhag to stand comfortably, but it would be a snug fit if we both wanted to lie down with some space in between us. Still, it was better than the atrium of the hollow tree above. The chii clearly didn't use this cave for anything, so we wouldn't get in the way.

Vruhag said something in his guttural language and the chii male chittered angrily in response.

"What are they saying?" I asked Ali'quii.

That's for them to say. Her mental voice sounded cheeky. *We will leave you to it. My Chosen and I have some acquainting to do.*

I didn't want to think too hard what that *acquainting* would look like.

"Please, can you stay for a bit and translate for me?

He understands what I'm saying, but not the other way round."

For a short while. We shall enter a mind room. Sit down and close your eyes.

I did as commanded. Vruhag did the same next to me. Our thighs touched. I scurried backwards, away from him, until I leaned against the mossy wall. A glow erupted around me, bathing Vruhag in turquoise light. In the narrow cave, only inches separated us. I could smell him. It was a scent unlike any other. Cinnamon mixed with pepper and fresh grass. No, honey and milk and cardamom. No, aniseed and petrichor. His scent was hard to pin down, yet it was deliciously attractive. I started breathing through my mouth to avoid smelling him, but even so, his closeness was electrifying. A shiver ran down my back and it was not an unpleasant one.

Why did he have this effect on me? Why did my core throb at the thought of our thighs touching?

Close your eyes, Ali'quii reminded me. I did so and tried to focus on something other than Vruhag's nearness.

A single dot of light flickered to life deep within my mind. I followed it, watching it become larger, until I suddenly sat in a brightly lit room. Wait, not a room. It was the tree above us, but even bigger and drenched in ethereal light.

Ali'quii and Ano'quoo sat in the centre of the tree atrium, their tails entwined. It had to be one of the cutest things I'd ever seen.

I sensed a presence behind me and turned around. Vruhag approached, his dynamic gait that of a predator. His wounds had disappeared, but some of the old scars remained. I was tempted to lift my shirt and check if my own scars were still there. Oh, I was wearing a shirt. No more moss wrap. It was my favourite green wrap top, paired with white jeans that I knew lay at the bottom of my wardrobe drawer back home. I'd last worn them to a date, an awful date with a guy who'd felt entitled to push his tongue down my throat after the first drink. I'd quickly taught him otherwise, but hadn't tried online dating after. Strange that my subconscious had dressed me in them now. Was it a warning or an encouragement?

I sat cross-legged opposite the two chii, while Vruhag kneeled to my right. He wore the same brown kilt as in real life, but he now had straps and holsters wrapped around his shoulders and arms. A knife glinted from a bone sheath strapped around his forearm, while the pendants on his necklace suspiciously looked like teeth or fangs. He oozed strength and uninhibited power.

"Can you understand me now?" he asked, his deep voice echoing through my mind. I didn't hear him with my ears, but with my heart.

"Yes, I can."

He smiled at me, and my mouth went dry. It was a sinful smile, full of desire and promises. He shouldn't smile at me like that. Not when we were strangers.

"Tell me why we're here. Tell me how to get home," I demanded.

His smile disappeared in an instant. "This planet is called Kalumbu," he began slowly, as if not sure what to tell me and what to sugar coat. "In simple terms, it's an arena. Cameras watch everything we do. The show is broadcast on hidden channels across the galaxy. Contestants are sent here to fight for survival. If they are still alive after ten rotations, they are taken to safety."

"How long is a rotation?" I asked at the same time as Ali'quii muttered, "Wrong."

Vruhag's attention snapped to the chii. "What?"

"They're not safe." For the first time, Ali'quii moved her lips while speaking. "I've seen them. They're lifted on a floating platform, high into the sky, then they're pushed over the rim. They fall. They crash. They die."

A barrage of emotions ran across Vruhag's face. He was so expressive. Or was I just particularly attuned to him? It felt easy to read what he was feeling even though he wasn't human.

"Are you sure?" he asked hoarsely.

Ano'quoo's tufted ears lowered. "I have seen it as well. Nobody ever leaves here alive. The beasts feast on them, whether they're alive or dead. The forest feeds off its sacrifices."

A series of shivers ran down my back and this time, they weren't the pleasant kind.

Vruhag looked at me, his eyes hooded. The spark in

his eyes extinguished as all hope seemed to flee him. The room turned cold.

"You said you have a way off this planet," I said weakly.

"I nodded," he muttered. "In my culture, that means no. I'm a captive just like you. I was abducted from my ship. My only hope was that we'd survive for ten rotations and finish the Trials that way. Ten rotations, that's ten cycles of day and night. We haven't even been here for one. And now it turns out we will die anyway, no matter if we somehow make it to the end of the Trials."

He sounded so defeated. If this warrior, this beast of a man, didn't see a way out, then what hope was there?

I wrapped my arms around my chest. "What do we do?"

He gave me a grim look. "We fight for as long as we can. Until the day the planet kills us."

14
VRUHAG

The cold shards of broken hopes littered my heart. It had been silly to trust the game makers, I knew that now. They had to give us hope, had to give us something to aim for. Contestants might just give up from the start if they knew they'd die anyway. Thrown from a platform to splatter on the ground. I'd rather die in battle, fighting the inevitable, my blood hot with rage.

I looked at my mate, her face pale as a corpse, foreshadowing the future. I'd only just found her. The game makers had given me my mate, dangled her in front of me as an incentive to perform like a trained animal, and now they were going to take her away again. It should have made me angry, but instead, icy despair was all I felt. What was the point of fighting, of surviving a few more rotations? For now, we were safe in the chii's cave, but I'd heard the rakefang's howl, I'd smelled several other predators in the vicinity. I'd keep them at bay for as long as I could, but once the game makers saw that the planet's natural predators weren't enough to kill us, they'd drop other contestants in this area. They wouldn't stop until we gave them what they wanted: an entertaining, bloody death.

"Is there no way out?" Fay asked feebly, her previous spunk gone. Just like my own confidence.

"You can stay with us," Ali'quii offered. "We can extend this cave, make it big enough for you to live in. When danger comes close, you can use our portals to travel to other chii tribes and seek refuge there."

I nodded. "We would put you all in danger. That's unacceptable."

"We know how to fight them," Ano'quoo hissed angrily, as if I'd offended his honour. "How do you think we're still alive? We stay hidden and fight from the shadows. We protect our own."

My wrist itched where his golden tail markings now sat.

Our own.

I inclined my head to the male, regretting our earlier fight. "I thank you for your kindness. I didn't mean to offend you. But they won't stop hunting us. I've watched the Trials. They're out for blood. People will have bet money on how long we survive, how we get killed. They will want to see our death. If we don't deliver that, there will be an outcry."

"Then we give it to them," Fay said slowly. "We give them a show. We pretend to fight each other, pretend to die. Afterwards we stay hidden in this cave for a while until they believe we really are dead."

I nodded again. "It won't work. It's a good idea, but they wouldn't believe we'd ever attack each other."

"Why not?"

Did she really not know or did she refuse to believe? Refuse to feel our bond?

"Because we are mates. They must have tested us on the space station. I've seen them do that before, they find mates and then drop them on Kalumbu together for extra drama."

She blinked, her expression hard to read. "What does that even mean?"

"You don't have mates in your world?"

She shook her head and I had to remind myself that it meant no. This was going to confuse me again and again.

"Theoretically, everyone has a mate - or mates - waiting for them somewhere in the universe. Mates are the perfect partners, complimenting each other in ways only mates can. But because mates can be on different planets, from different species, only some ever find each other. That's what makes the bond even more special."

"What if they don't like each other?"

I sucked in a sharp breath. "That never happens. As I said, mates are perfect for each other. Of course, any couple will have difficult moments, but the mate bond is something sacred, something deep, that always pulls them back together."

"Always?" she asked softly.

"Always. Mates are forever. Some species can't

survive without their mate. Others will go crazy if they can't be with their mate."

I didn't say that I belonged to the latter. I didn't want to scare her, didn't want to put pressure on her. I may have looked like a battle-hardened warrior on the outside, but I was a big softie inside. I believed in love, in romance. I wanted her to fall for me. I wanted to seduce her until she could no longer deny the truth. Yet the mating fever would make that difficult. The urge to pounce on her was getting stronger. Every time her scent filled my nostrils, my shaft swelled with desire.

"I don't believe it," Fay said firmly. "I'm human. How can I be your...mate? I don't even know what you are."

"I'm an orc from the planet Orcadia," I replied, fighting the dismay at hearing her words. She'd change her mind. I'd make sure she would.

"I thought orcs were a creature from mythology and fantasy novels," she muttered. "How can this be? How can you be real?"

"Your subconscious may have chosen a word already in your vocabulary, since you lack the terms to describe my species. Once you have a translator implant, you'll hear the official translation."

Her brow furrowed. "I don't want an implant. I don't want anything alien inside me. The thought of that...no, it's wrong."

Fear flickered behind her eyes. I couldn't imagine what she'd been through. Taken from her planet before her species was even aware of the existence of aliens. It all had to be terribly frightening. Yet it wouldn't get any easier for her, not on Kalumbu. I had a feeling that it had only just begun.

"Anyway, what's the plan?" Fay asked. "What do we do now? We can't stay in this cave forever. I need to get home."

Reality still hadn't sunk in for her. She still had hope. I couldn't take that from her. Hope might keep her alive for longer.

"I need to find out more about where we are," I hedged. "Scout the area. Discover what kind of tech the chii have access to."

"We don't have our own technology," Ano'quoo interrupted. "We use that the ancients left behind, but once it fails, we can't repair it."

He sounded annoyed that he had to admit to it.

"You can stay with us for as long as you like," Ali'quii said in her melodic voice, much nicer than Ano'quoo's grumbly tone. "Our tribe will be pleased to accommodate you. We can extend this cave, turn it into a home. We will have to explore which of our foods suit you, but the forest provides. You can survive here. With us."

She didn't understand that the game makers wouldn't let us be. None of them did. But because I didn't want to alarm my mate, I stayed silent. For now, we could stay. I could try and learn my mate's language so that we could communicate without the chiis' help. We could get to know each other. Complete the mate bond. Until the day they'd come for us.

There had to be another option. Some other way. But my mind was blank. I was a warrior, not a strategist.

"Will anyone search for you?" Fay suddenly asked me. "Do you have a family?"

I nodded, then shook my head to adjust to her Peritan gestures. "Not anymore. I'm a mercenary, fighting for whoever pays the most. I was on the way to a job when they captured my ship, but I doubt the general who hired me will send out search parties." I laughed at the thought. General Xylow would probably be glad to never see my face again. He despised having to rely on my skills, yet his soldiers were no match for me. They were little lordlings and soft adolescents who didn't know which end of an axe cut off an enemy's head. Xylow had hired me many times before, but when I didn't show up, he'd assume I'd found a better job.

"Nobody will come looking for me," I said into the silence. "We're on our own."

"You have us," Ano'quoo interjected, glaring at me. I didn't understand the little male. He was cold and abrupt one moment, yet he had helped me, healed me, and clearly didn't want us to leave.

"You do," Ali'quii confirmed and gave her Chosen a warm smile. "We will retreat to our new room in the tree, giving you some time to get to know each other."

"But I won't be able to understand what he says," Fay protested.

Ali'quii curled her tails around my mate's wrist.

Her golden mark looked almost identical to mine. "You are mates, whether you accept it or not. Listen to your heart. You will understand him if you listen."

The room around us faded without warning, replaced by the dim light of the cave. The two chii left without another word, their tails entwined. They'd only just met yet they already looked like they were utterly in love. I shot a glance at my mate. She'd wrapped her arms around her legs, her eyes downcast, her expression gloomy.

My heart hurt at the pain and fear she was clearly feeling. I wanted her to be happy. Wanted her to be in my arms, safe and sound.

A curse tumbled from my lips and I was glad she couldn't understand me. My mother would have clapped my ears for using such language in the presence of my mate.

"What did you say?" Fay asked without looking at me.

I didn't respond. Didn't know what to say. Instead, I lay on the hard floor and patted my chest. My head and feet touched the cave walls, but Fay would be able to stretch out comfortably. For once, her small stature was an advantage.

She stared at me, lifting her head as she took in my body. I patted my chest again, an invitation.

"If you think I'm going to sleep on top of you, you're insane," she muttered. "I'm fine where I am."

She closed her eyes as if to demonstrate that she could sleep in that ridiculous position. Did Peritans sleep while sitting? It could be possible, but it didn't look comfortable.

As much as I wanted to pull her close, I let her be. I closed my eyes as well, pretending to sleep, but I knew I'd find no rest until she was curled up by my side.

I waited and waited.

After a small eternity, she moved, lying next to me, but making sure not to touch me. The cave was so narrow that it was an achievement in itself. She had to be lying on her side to fit into the remaining space. Only a tusk's width separated us. I could feel her warmth. All it would take was one movement, one arm extended to feel her, touch her, claim her...

But I stayed as I was, stiff as a board, while listening to the soft sound of her breathing.

15
FAY

I was too warm. I dimly remembered being cold during the night, the icy cave floor sucking all the warmth from me, but now I was hot. Too much so. And the cave was no longer hard, my hips no longer hurting.

I breathed in deep, pushing away the remnants of sleep tugging at my thoughts. Waking up was hard. I dimly knew that reality wasn't going to be pleasant, but at the same time, sleep was just a temporary reprieve. I'd had nightmares. I couldn't remember them, but the clammy feeling was still there.

The warm ground shifted beneath me and I had to admit to what I already knew.

I was lying on top of an orc.

I didn't dare to move. Didn't want to wake him. Once he calmed again, I might be able to roll off ever so slowly, with him being none the wiser once he woke up.

But then he chuckled and I knew he was awake. He

whispered something in his guttural language. Again, I thought how the sound of his orc language matched his rugged exterior. He could have been reciting poetry, for all I knew, but it made me think of battles and barbarians and something feral, primitive.

He continued talking, clearly not expecting an answer, not expecting me to understand. Was he telling me a story?

My right arm itched. I wanted to scratch, but that would have been admitting that I was awake. He already knew, but still.

His monologue was making me drift back towards sleep. If only he hadn't been so hot. It was like lying on a heater. I needed to cool down before I started to drip sweat all over him. I grit my teeth and took a deep breath. Time for the day to begin.

I rolled off him as fast as I could until I hit the cold wall to my right. Blue light flashed all around me as I activated the strange moss. That reminded me that all I was wearing was my moss wrap. It had slipped down a bit during the night, enough to show some cleavage, but mercifully my boobs were still covered.

Vruhag chuckled and said something. I didn't want to know what it was. His voice sounded teasing, almost saucy. I got to my feet and pulled up my moss wrap. A shiver ran over my skin. It was cold in the cave, now that I was no longer a recipient of the orc's body heat. I'd have to ask Ali'quii if she knew of an alternative clothing to moss. It wasn't going to last much longer, already falling apart at the edges. If I was going to die on this planet, I didn't want to do so naked. Strange priorities, maybe, but in the end it was all about dignity.

The orc said something more.

"I don't understand you, stop talking," I snapped, regretting it a moment later when his expression fell. He looked like a wounded puppy. Oh my. "Sorry," I muttered. "I'm grumpy in the morning. Especially when waking up on a distant planet with no clothes, no tea and no books."

I can help with the tea.

Ali'quii's voice sounded in my head a moment before I could hear her paw steps as she entered the cave. Her Chosen wasn't with her, but the little chii positively glowed with happiness. I didn't want to imagine what her and Ano'quoo had been up to last night.

What are books?

Taken aback, it took me a moment to respond. "Books are...how do I describe them? Lots of sheets of paper bound together. Wait, do you have a written language? Can you write?"

Ali'quii cocked her feathered head to one side.

I understand the concept through our link, but no, we don't. We draw. We tell stories. We listen to the ancestors in our dreams.

No books. Not a single book for the rest of my life. The thought scared me almost more than faceless aliens wanting us to die a violent death. Living wasn't all about surviving. I needed more than just food and shelter.

A heavy hand landed on my shoulder. Vruhag smiled down at me, then nodded pointedly.

"You have books?" I asked, hoping I was interpreting his nod correctly.

His grin widened and he said something, putting emphasis on sounds I didn't think my tongue and vocal cords could replicate.

He says that he knows what books are, Ali'quii translated. *He promises to take you to one of the Intergalactic University's public libraries.*

She stumbled over the words, clearly not knowing what a library was.

I looked into Vruhag's moss-green eyes. "Thank you."

I knew he didn't mean it. I knew we'd likely never get off this planet. And even if we did, all I wanted was to go home, back to Earth.

We have made food for you. Come.

We followed Ali'quii out of the cave. It was hard to tell how late in the morning it was. The canopy blocked the view of the sun, but it was starting to get warm and humid in the forest.

"Is there a patch of this moss somewhere nearby?" I asked the chii while walking back to the tree's main entrance. "I need something I can turn into clothes."

Clothes? Picture it in your mind, she commanded.

Ah yes, the advantage of being covered in feathers. The chii had no need for clothes. I randomly pictured a sun dress, then a t-shirt with loose linen trousers, then a more form-fitting evening dress that I'd once bought on a whim and never actually worn. I finished my mental runway with a winter outfit complete with a thick down coat.

I have something better than moss. After morning meal.

A crowd of about two dozen chii awaited us in front of the tree. They each carried a bowl or dish laden with food. Some of it was clearly fruit and berries, other things were harder to identify. My stomach growled as I realised it was now at least an entire day since I'd last eaten. Ali'quii had given me teas and juices to try yesterday, but then Vruhag and Ano'quoo had arrived and I'd forgotten all about food.

Sit. We will give you things to try, then you say what you like and we will get bigger portions.

She'd need to get *very* big portions for Vruhag. The tiny bowls the chii were carrying wouldn't even be enough for a single mouthful for the orc. I hoped we wouldn't empty the chii's foodstores during our stay with them. Yet another reason why we couldn't live with them forever. Their world wasn't made for humanoids, especially not one as huge as Vruhag.

We sat down in front of their tree home. The orc's knee touched mine until I scurried back. He shot me a disappointed glance, but I ignored him. The sooner he understood that I was not interested in being his mate, the better.

Ali'quii chirped and the chii queued up in two

lines, one for each of us. The male chii at the front of my queue puffed up his feathers in self-importance as he handed me a tiny bowl filled with a green mush. I dipped my finger into it, expecting it to taste like peas, but almost spat it out again when a rancid taste filled my mouth.

"Not for me," I told Ali'quii, fighting hard against the urge to throw up. I didn't want to be impolite. The chii were trying so hard to make us feel welcome.

The next two dishes were okay, edible but nothing I'd eat for pleasure, but the tiny green balls an elderly female chii handed me were spectacular. Flavour exploded in my mouth, something that reminded me of a good korma curry back home. The balls looked like leaves mushed together, but whatever they really were, I could easily eat a whole plate of them. A *human-sized* plate, not the chii version.

I felt like I was being watched by more than just the curious chii. I looked up and met Vruhag's amused glance. He said something in his guttural language and Ali'quii chittered in response.

He wants to know what it is so he can feed it to you in future, she translated for me. *He says he can't get enough of your pleased expression. I will give him the recipe, if you want.*

Somehow, I guessed that 'pleased expression' wasn't the term Vruhag had used. Heat rose to my cheeks. To overplay my embarrassment, I handed him the last of my green curry balls.

"You try one," I said.

His eyes widened in surprise. Had something got lost in translation again? That wasn't a normal reaction to someone offering you food.

With his gaze roaming my face, my body, he put one hand on his chest and said something.

He accepts, Ali'quii translated.

That sounded ominous.

"Uhm, you know I only gave you some food to try, right? There's no deeper meaning to that. At least not for me."

Something flashed across his face, too fast to read. Then he inclined his head and bit into the ball.

In some cultures, it's a sign of deep affection when a female gives her male food, Ali'quii told me. *I don't know if it's the same for Vruhag, but from his reaction, I'd guess so.*

Great. Now he thought I was leading him on.

For the rest of the meal, I avoided looking at the orc. I ate until I was full, then enjoyed a cup of fruit juice that had to be carried by two chii. I didn't know where they'd found a wooden mug that was almost bigger than what I would have used at home, but I was touched by the effort they put into it. None of the other dishes were as good as the curry balls, but some came close. I would have pocketed some leaf strips that looked as if they'd been dunked in honey and tasted like vanilla, if I'd had pockets. That was going to be my next project. Clothes. Ali'quii had said that she had something better than the moss I currently wore. I didn't want to get my hopes up just yet, but please,

please could it be some woven fabric rather than leaves or yet more moss?

Without warning, Vruhag growled and launched himself into the air, jumping higher than I would have thought possible. His fist clenched around something and a crack echoed through the stunned silence. All eyes were on the orc. The chii looked scared, although I wasn't sure if they were afraid of Vruhag or whatever he'd caught.

Fury blazing in his eyes, he turned to me and opened his palm. Small pieces of metal and wires. It was hard to guess the original shape after he'd crushed it.

"What is it?" I asked, but I already knew the answer.

"Camera drone," he grunted. "They know where we are. We're no longer safe here."

16
VRUHAG

I'd hoped we'd have more time in this peaceful oasis, but it wasn't to be. At least we'd managed to get some sleep and food before the camera drones had found us. How long until the game makers sent predators or other contestants to this location? I'd destroyed the drone as soon as I'd spotted it, but I knew they transmitted live. They had seen us, no doubt about it.

I held out a hand to my mate who was still sitting on the forest floor.

"We have to go," I said, regretting that I had to take her away. Out in the forest, we'd have no chii to cook and translate for us. We'd be on our own. No shelter. No allies. The only weapon the axe on my belt. And Fay was so vulnerable. I would have worried for her even if she'd worn full-body armour, but she was practically naked.

Last night, when she'd rolled on top of me, I'd stopped breathing. Her skin had been cool against mine and I'd done my best to warm her without waking her. I'd increased my metabolism to generate extra heat, not caring that it would eat into my reserves. She'd moaned softly in her sleep, a sound so sweet that my shaft had ached with desire. I wanted her to make that sound for me, just for me.

I'd barely slept, too aware of her half-naked body draped over my chest. She barely weighed anything. Were all Peritan females this way or was she particularly small? At one point, when my shaft had strained against the leather kilt, I'd wondered if I'd fit into her. But we were mates, made for each other. The stars had led us together. I'd never heard of mates who weren't physically compatible.

"Where are we going?" Fay said and ignored my hand, jumping to her feet without my help.

"As far away as possible. I want to go through a portal, if the chii will guide us to one," I said and waited for Ali'quii to translate.

Ano'quoo climbed onto my shoulder and wrapped his feathered tails around my neck. If any other male had done that, he'd be dead already. But Ano'quoo was special, no matter how annoying the little beastie could be.

I will take you to a portal that leads to a distant place. Nobody leaves near there any more, but there are ruins where you can seek shelter. My Chosen will prepare supplies for you.

Ali'quii had already run off, taking half the chii with her.

"Thank you. You should stay on your guard. I don't know if the game makers are interested in you. They might take you for simple animals and ignore you, but if they suspect that you are more than that, they might come for you."

Don't worry. We have ways to defend ourselves. We know their ways. We have watched them for a long time, preparing for the day they'd see us as a threat. We are ready.

I really hoped they were. If I didn't have Fay to think about, I would have stayed and defended them myself. But our presence here likely brought them more danger than protection. We had to leave.

We will leave supplies at the portal every few sunrises, Ano'quoo promised. *And even if you can't see us, we will be watching.*

"Thank you, my friend," I said and meant it. Ano'quoo may be insufferable, but his heart was in the right place. And maybe his Chosen would drive away some of his arrogance over time. Females could have that effect on males.

Ali'quii returned, huffing and puffing under the weight of the leaf-covered bundles she was carrying. A handful of chii behind here were similarly laden.

She turned to my mate, but spoke in both our minds. *The clan mother wants to talk to you before you leave. Come inside. Your mate has to stay out here. This is between females only.*

"We need to leave soon," I warned, but they ignored me. Fay followed Ali'quii into the tree, ducking her head as she passed through the opening. I was curious about what they were hiding within the tree, but I was likely too large to even fit through the entrance.

The chii dropped their bundles at my feet. I ripped one of the leather straps from my kilt and used it to tie them together until I could carry them all with one hand. Not ideal if I had to fight, but at least we had food.

"Do you have anything we can use to carry water?" I asked Ano'quoo.

Our carvers are making you large bottles as we speak, he replied testily, as if I was asking the obvious.

"Thank you."

His tails tightened around my neck in response. More chii came running with supplies and I had to use another kilt strap to turn them into a bundle. This should last us several days, if I only ate as much as my mate.

With every click that passed without Fay coming out of the tree, I grew more impatient. Every moment we remained with the chii was dangerous for both them and us. Ano'quoo seemed to sense my irritation.

You cannot hurry the clan mother. His mental voice was full of amusement. *She would take her time in the middle of a lightning storm. Be patient. There is a reason for the delay.*

I didn't ask what that reason was. They hadn't wanted me in there. This was something for females, which meant it probably involved embarrassing things that would make my ears turn dark if I listened to them. No, it was good that I was outside with Ano'quoo.

I looked at the chii on my shoulder. "If we don't see each other again... I hope you have a wonderful life with your Chosen. Thank you for your help."

He wriggled his nose. *This is not the end. We will see each other again.*

As much as I wanted to, I didn't share his optimism. Fay and I were about to be hunted. It was unlikely we would survive for long. I just wished that we'd die as true mates, with our bond intact. A horrible thought struck me. Would we find each other in the afterlife if we hadn't completed the bond? A sense of urgency filled me. I had to mate with Fay. Had to make her see that it was important. I'd only just found her. If the game makers succeeded in killing us, I wanted to know that at least we'd have eternity together in the afterlife.

For a moment, I considered that this might be the mating fever messing with my head, but no, this was real. A true concern that I had to deal with. Once we'd relocated to somewhere safer, the ruins Ano'quoo had mentioned, I'd claim my mate. Make her truly mine. Forever.

A growl escaped me at the same time as Fay stepped out of the giant tree. I noticed the curious look she gave me, but then my gaze wandered down and I saw what she was wearing. My breath fled as my shaft grew rock hard. I had to clench my fists to stop me from pouncing at her.

She was a dream. Wore a dream, a wet dream

that would stay with me forever. The chii had clad her in a dress woven from lilac vines. It was fastened around her neck with a thick blue vine and reached down to just above her knees. I didn't know if they'd made a loose weave because they had to hurry or because that was their way of working with the vines, but I was grateful to them. The dress showed more than it concealed. I could see her smooth skin through the holes in the fabric, the mounds of her breast, the...

I quickly lifted my gaze again. If I looked at her crotch for too long, I'd lose control.

My mate was stunningly beautiful in that dress. Yet she didn't seem to be aware of it.

She cocked her head, looking at me in confusion. "Why are you staring at me like that?"

I couldn't respond. Didn't have the words.

All I wanted was to lick her. Kiss her. Claim her.

The mating fever roared within me. It was hard to resist, so hard. My skin was aflame with desire.

I forced myself to turn around, away from her.

"Let's go," I said brusquely and grabbed the two bundles.

Ano'quoo chittered something to his Chosen. It sounded like he was amused. I ignored him.

It was rude to walk away without saying goodbye to the chii. But it would be even ruder if I claimed my mate in front of them all. The urge was so strong. Was this the mating fever or something else?

I heard her footsteps behind me, heavier than

usual. She was also carrying something, but I couldn't get myself to look around. I didn't have the self-control.

With Fay and probably Ali'quii following me, I walked back to the portal Ano'quoo and I had come through yesterday. The chii didn't correct my direction, so I assumed that it would be able to take us to the place he'd mentioned. It was going to be interesting to see how their portal technology worked. The simplest portals were linked to only one other, offering fast but inflexible travel. More advanced tech could switch between several destinations, if their programming matched that of the receiving portal. Since this technology wasn't of chii origin but something older, I'd assumed it was fairly basic.

The forest was quiet this morning. I felt the gaze of animals on me, high up in the canopy, but they were prey watching me with worry. I couldn't sense any predators nearby. Whatever had howled last night had moved on. For now. I bet several camera drones were on the way here to replace the one I'd destroyed. If we were lucky, we'd get to the portal before they arrived.

"Can you walk a bit slower?" Fay called softly. Her breath was loud and fast. "My legs aren't as long as yours."

I grimaced, angry at myself for not considering her smaller statue. Yes, we were in a hurry, but I didn't want her to exhaust herself just yet.

Without a response, I slowed my pace while keeping my focus on her breathing until it slowed down to a steadier rhythm.

Go right here, Ano'quoo instructed when we were only a few clicks from the portal. *Through the gap in the trees and then up the hill.*

Not the same portal after all. I followed his instructions, slowing down further when we got to a steep slope. The trees here were smaller than the ones we'd passed, but still much taller than any we had on Orcadia. Their bark looked strangely furry and I was tempted to stroke one of them, but this was Kalumbu. The bark was likely poisonous. Everything here was out to kill us. Everything except the chii. Finding them had been a miracle.

By the time we got to the portal, the sun had almost reached its zenith. I was thirsty and could have devoured half a rakefang. Breakfast felt like a long time ago - and it hadn't been sufficient. I'd been too busy observing my mate as she'd tried chii dishes. It had been the best entertainment I'd had in ages. Her face was so expressive. Whenever she'd eaten something she didn't like, her lips quivered and tiny wrinkles appeared between her eyes, but she always smoothed her expression so as not to offend the chii. It had been amusing to watch.

Stop, Ano'quoo commanded and jumped off me, landing elegantly on all fours. He used his two tails to point north. *The portal is just behind these bushes. We will leave you now, but we will bring supplies here regularly. I hope you'll find a safe place.*

"Thank you for leading us here," Fay said. He must

have spoken to both of our minds at once. "I really appreciate all your help."

I finally turned around to her. She was cradling Ali'quii in her arms as if she didn't want to let go of the chii female. Ali'quii's tails were wrapped around Fay's wrist, exactly where the mark was.

If you need help, touch your marks together and speak our names, Ali'quii said softly. *We will come if you call.*

I rubbed my mark, dubious what else it might be able to do. Would it ever fade? I likely wouldn't live long enough to find out.

Fay sat Ali'quii onto the ground and clutched her bundle to her chest instead. I'd not noticed what she was carrying before, but it looked like two wooden bottles in a net carrier, large enough to sate even my thirst.

The two chii sat side by side, their tails entwined. They looked as if they'd been together forever, not just a single day. My heart ached at the sight. I wanted it to be the same with Fay. Wanted her to snuggle against my side, where she belonged. But instinct told me that pulling her close would have the opposite effect. I had to wait until she came to me. For the first time in my life, I decided to be patient.

"I guess I'm ready," Fay said to me. "Let's find out where this portal leads."

I shook my head, then nodded when I remembered it would look wrong to her.

With one last look at the chii couple, I stepped

around the bushes. The air between two ancient trees shimmered and sparkled; the only sign that this was the location of the portal. I held out a hand to my mate.

To my surprise, she took it, and together, we stepped through the portal.

17

FAY

This time, I'd been prepared for the pain, but instead of feeling like I was being torn apart, I only experienced an irritating itch all over my body. When my feet hit solid ground, I swayed, but managed to stay upright. Holding Vruhag's hand helped with balance; not that I would have admitted that to his face. He groaned, his face a paler shade of green. He looked like he was about to throw up.

I was rather happy that I'd weathered the portal better than him. Not that it was a competition. But still, it was nice to beat this huge, muscly orc at something.

A bird's call made me look up. The trees were just as tall here, seeming to reach all the way to the clouds, hiding the sun from view. There was movement in the canopy. Hopefully just birds and critters, not something wanting to eat us. I assumed Vruhag, who'd proven he had more astute senses, would warn me before something leapt from the heights. Then I remembered our language barrier. Well, I supposed I'd recognise a shout of alarm from a shout of joy. His expressions certainly seemed close enough to those I was used to from other humans.

Other humans. I'd never thought of myself as *human*, as in a sentient species that was among other sentient species. I'd called myself a journalist, British, a woman, but not human. My profession no longer mattered. Neither did my nationality. My gender only because Vruhag thought I was his mate. Priorities had shifted and I didn't think I liked it.

Vruhag said something in a low voice to attract my attention. He walked through the stone gate in front of us, expecting me to follow. Nature had reclaimed whatever this place had once been. Vines and moss covered huge stone blocks that had once been part of walls, while trees grew on top of them, their roots clinging to the polished stone. Whoever had lived here had left long, long ago.

The gate was tall enough for two Vrughags. After the miniature world of the chii, this was the exact opposite. We were in the playground of giants.

I hurried after the orc but stopped after just a few steps. I felt my mouth open as I took in the landscape around us. Beyond the gate was carnage. This wasn't a city that had been abandoned over time. It had been ransacked, destroyed, ground to dust. The few remaining walls bore marks of battle, with holes that spoke of missiles and explosions. A shiver ran down my back. The civilisation who'd lived here had been advanced enough to build the portals. Whoever had forced them to extinction must have been extremely powerful. What would they do to Earth if they came there? We wouldn't stand a chance.

Vruhag and I didn't stand a chance. We were only putting off the inevitable.

My eyes burned as I gazed upon the signs of destruction. The ruins spread over at least half a mile before the forest grew too dense to see them. There must have been thousands of people here. And now they were all gone, the only sign they ever existed some smoothly polished stones and the stories the chii told.

"Fay," Vruhag said. I liked the way he pronounced my name. It made it sound kickarse rather than soft and mythical.

"Yes?"

His attention was on my eyes, my traitorous, leaking eyes. He slowly reached out as if to wipe away my tears, but I stepped back and rubbed my eyes. I called on the steel within me, the strength that had got me to survive in warzones. I locked away all emotion and ignored the pain that seemed to seep from the ruins.

"Let's find shelter," I said, my voice cold. "Maybe there's a building that still has a roof."

It didn't seem likely, not with the extent of the destruction, but Vruhag gave me a court nod and turned to the left.

"You go left, I go right and we call if we find something," I suggested.

The orc whirled around and snarled at me.

I stared at him in surprise. "What's wrong?"

He grunted something incomprehensible. If I'd had the patience, I would have used yes and no question to find out what he was saying, but I didn't care.

I sighed. "Stay together?"

He nodded vehemently.

"Alright. Then we shall both go left."

He held out a hand and I pointedly ignored it. This wasn't the place to walk around hand in hand like a lovesick couple. His presence distracted me. Touching him would only make it worse. Besides, I'd noticed something on the walk to the portal that had sent a whole whirlwind of emotions through me. I'd been glad we'd walked there in silence so I could sort out my feelings.

When I'd first noticed, I'd bent down to remove a piece of bark from between my toes. Yet even though I hadn't looked at him, I'd been able to *feel* him. I'd known exactly where he was standing. It was as if he'd turned into an extension of my own body. I didn't have to look at my hand just now to know it was gripping the wooden bottles the chii had given me. And I didn't have to look at Vruhag to know where he was, how he moved, how he felt.

I gasped. That was new.

The emotion spilling into me wasn't my own. The trepidation, the worry, the adoration.

"What the fuck?" I exclaimed. "What have you done to me?"

Vruhag frowned at me and asked something in return. Of course, I didn't understand a word. It only made me angrier.

For a moment, I wondered if he could feel my emotions, my anger, but then I pushed that thought aside. I didn't care.

"Get out of my mind," I growled. "I don't want to feel you. I don't want to know how big your body is, how you walk with legs like tree trunks, how your senses are focused on me-"

I clasped a hand over my mouth to stop the words from tumbling out. It sounded pathetic. I was probably imagining it all. This couldn't be real. I couldn't sense his tight grip around the leather strap, the pain in his chest as he looked at me, the pain further down where he strained against his kilt-like garment...

I turned away from him, unwilling to let him see me. I felt *everything*. And it was all too much.

"Go away," I whispered. "Please."

But he didn't.

He said something in a warm, soothing voice. I didn't think he could sound that...soft. It made it almost worse. He was a good guy, I had no doubts about that. If we'd met in a bar, I may have taken him home for some no-strings-attached fun. But I *felt* him. Like he was part of me. And that was an invasion into my mind, into my heart. I needed him to stop it. I didn't want to know that he was worried about me just now. That he was wondering whether this was my own kind of mating fever.

Wait.

This was more than just emotions. I was sensing his thoughts.

For a second, that thrilled me - I'd be able to understand him now - before reality wrapped its cold fingers around my throat. This was not a good thing. Who knew what would come next. Would he be able to hear my own thoughts? I'd have no privacy. No solitude. Would I have nowhere left to go that was truly mine? He'd know everything. Knew about my past. About the mistakes I'd made. About my weaknesses. My fears. And he'd know about the struggle that I'd kept contained deep within my heart ever since we'd met.

Had it only been yesterday? For some reason, it felt like I'd known him for longer.

"What's happening?" I asked, my voice choked and pathetic.

He spoke in his guttural language, but at the same time, I felt the meaning of his words. I didn't hear him with my ears nor my mind. I heard him in my heart.

"The mating bond is getting volatile. If we don't commit to it soon, my mating fever will get worse and for you... I don't know what this is. It must be how your species reacts to mates."

I laughed harshly. "My species doesn't have mates. This is all some alien humbug that I'm trying to escape."

"But why?" His sadness hurt me. "Why are you fighting the bond? I am not a bad person. I will make you happy. I will protect you from our enemies. I will die fighting for you."

"But I don't want you to," I snapped. "I want to make my own choices. I don't want some magical bond to dictate who I'm with. I want to fall in love with my Prince Charming without someone telling me that he's the one. I just want a normal life, is that too much to ask?"

I looked around the alien ruins. Yes, it was. I'd never live a normal life again. Even if I somehow made it back to Earth, I couldn't forget all the things I'd seen. Aliens were real. Could I simply return to my old life, ignoring that there was an entire galaxy of the unknown out there? I was a journalist not just by profession, but by calling. I'd always asked too many questions. I'd always thirsted for knowledge.

The realisation that there was no going back to my old life was bitter and painful.

A large hand settled on my shoulder.

"I'm sorry," Vruhag said ever so softly. "I don't want you to feel as if you don't have control. I can't even imagine how difficult it must be for you, abducted from your planet and thrown into the Trials while also finding your mate, but I will be with you every step of the way. I will walk by your side and I will carry you if you need me to. I will give you the space you need, but I have to warn you. The mating fever is getting stronger. I don't know how much longer I can control it."

"Tell me about this mating fever."

The more we spoke, the easier understanding him

became. His responses became like a second internal voice, feeling as natural as my own. It scared me.

"Do you really want to know?"

I just nodded.

"After an orc male first scents his female, his body prepares to claim her. If that process is interrupted or if the male doesn't claim his female as soon as he is ready, there are side effects. I-"

Without warning, he wrapped his arms around me and pulled me forwards. We fell, a controlled fall, and I landed on top of him. He'd moved faster than I could even begin to comprehend.

"What-"

He silenced me with a worried look. I tried to listen for whatever had alarmed him, but all I could hear was the chirping of birds high above us. Slowly, he moved us, crawling while keeping one arm around my waist, pressing me against him. He stopped when he had his back against a stone wall. Vines growing above us offered some shelter from prying eyes. We lay there in silence, waiting for whatever he'd heard to either pass or to find us.

His scent surrounded me like a comforting blanket. With all my senses on high alert, his presence was overwhelming. I didn't just feel him where our bodies touched, where my chest pressed against his. Through this strange bond, I also felt stones digging into his back, an old pain near his hip, and most embarrassingly of all, his erection. Despite the danger around us, he was aroused. I didn't fault him for it. My core clenched and throbbed, my breasts were taut and my nipples hard. I was reacting to him just like he was to me. I blamed the bond. This wasn't me. Wasn't natural. Yes, he was hot as fuck, despite the green skin and the tusks - or maybe because of them - but this was no way to feel in the middle of a life or death situation.

"Drones," he whispered. "At least three."

I still didn't hear anything besides our heavy breathing. The jungle had become quieter, less birds calling out above us.

Yet I trusted Vruhag to know how best to evade these drones. If that meant lying on the ground, so be it.

If only his scent hadn't been this strong. If only it hadn't made me want to brush my lips over his collarbone to see if he tasted like he smelled.

18

VRUHAG

Her arousal was dangerous for my sanity. Fay's scent was getting stronger with every click that passed. Physical proximity was a bad idea right now. It would be so easy to push up her woven dress and claim her. So, so easy.

A tiny voice, the only part of me that was clinging on to sanity, reminded me of the danger. I could hear three camera drones flying towards us. To send three drones meant other things were on the way as well. Things that would give the viewers the spectacle they were craving. I didn't know how they'd found us this quickly. I'd thought we'd have some time to find shelter, maybe even a whole day or two to gather our strength, explore the area, make weapons.

But it wasn't to be. They were coming.

This time, I doubted any of the drones would come close enough for me to crush it. They would have learned their lesson. They'd circle above us, filming whatever horrible things they'd planned for us.

Death was coming.

And I wasn't ready.

Far, far in the distance, something roared. Not a rakefang, but I didn't doubt that it would be at least as dangerous. The game makers had seen that I could handle several rakefangs at once. Granted, without Ano'quoo's help, I may not have fared as well, but I wasn't sure how much they knew about the chii. And this time, I had Fay to protect. They hadn't even given her a weapon. Dropped her onto the planet naked and unarmed. They'd either expected a quick death or had banked on me finding my mate. I didn't know which option was worse.

The first drone reached us, hovering high above us. I was tempted to throw a rock at it, but it would only give away our location. I hoped that the shadow of the wall paired with the undergrowth and vines hid us from the cameras. But it would be no defence against predators. I'd have to get up and fight, give the cameras what they wanted.

If Fay hadn't been with me, I would have made my last stand on one of the walls, in full sight. Give them the show the game makers were desperate for. Fight until the last breath. But I had my mate to think of. She was no warrior.

Maybe she could go back through the portal. I'd hold them back, give her time to run. But that would leave her without any protection once I was gone.

No, we would die together. I wouldn't let her out of my sight.

"Is this it?" Fay whispered.

"Maybe. It depends on who they've sent after us."

She looked at me, determination building within her. I could feel her intentions now. The bond was getting stronger.

"Then let's face them and fight," she said. Any orc would have been proud to hear their mate say such words, yet Fay was Peritan. Soft and tuskless. For her to have the strength of a warrior was exceptional.

"We might die."

Her eyes flickered fiercely. "Then so be it. They took me from my home. I won't lay here and wait for them to kill me. I want to fight."

And just like that, it was decided. She climbed off me and held out a hand. Just like I had done this very morning. With a smile, I grasped it and pretended to need her help while getting up. I picked up a large stick and used my axe to sharpen one end of it. The makeshift spear wouldn't last long, but it was better than nothing.

I handed it to Fay. She took it without a word and ran her hands over the shaft. She stabbed the air a few times to test the spear's weight. I smiled approvingly. Her body may have been soft, but her mind was that of a fighter.

"Let's find high ground," I said, "before the beasts reach us."

More howls had joined the first. They were getting

closer fast. At least four predators, likely more. And there may have been other contestants on their way as well, drawn by the noise of the beasts.

Not much longer now. But we hadn't completed the mating. Was our bond strong enough yet to lead us together in the afterlife? I prayed to my ancestors that it would. I couldn't imagine being without Fay. She was everything I'd dreamed of in a mate and more.

I scanned the ruins around us before settling on several large stone slabs surrounded by only light undergrowth. Once, they may have been the ceiling of a large room. We'd have a better view on top of the slabs and they were wide enough to give us a platform we could fight on.

I led my mate to the ruined building and helped her up onto the stone slabs. They were perfectly polished, still as smooth as when this had been a bustling settlement. For a moment, I let myself imagine the people who'd lived here, who'd died here. Today, I would try and avenge at least some of them.

Fay continued to stab some imaginary enemies, testing how far her spear could reach. If she was lucky, she could keep a beast engaged at a distance, holding it off until I could cut off its head.

A fearsome roar echoed through the forest. Above us, the birds had fallen deadly silent. The only animals still making a sound were the predators racing towards us. So close now. Only a click away.

I turned to my mate. "Would you allow me to kiss you?"

"Is that how you flirt? Wait until we're about to be eaten before popping the question?"

I took a step towards her. "I cannot imagine dying without having tasted you at least once."

Her full lips opened ever so slightly. The scent of her arousal was driving me crazy. She wanted this. I knew it, clear as the sacred pond of Batival.

"Yes," she breathed, barely a sound, yet enough for me.

I wrapped my arms around her, making sure the axe was pointing away from my mate, locked eyes with her one last time, then crushed my lips against hers.

It was nothing like I'd imagined. It was better, a thousand times better. She tasted of sweet nectar, of faraway planets, of life itself. Her lips were soft yet demanding as she leaned into the kiss, claiming me just as I was claiming her. I held her in my arms, savouring the feeling, committing it to memory.

This was the best moment of my life.

And it ended with a mighty roar.

A beast burst from the forest and into the clearing. With one last swipe of my tongue against her lips, so full of regret, so full of all the things that could have been, I turned to face our attacker.

It was huge. The rakefangs had been mere pups compared to this monster. A huge furry body balanced on eight spindly legs that ended in hooked claws. A barbed tail swung through the air as it approached menacingly. Its head consisted only of a huge maw large enough to swallow me whole. If it had eyes, I couldn't see them.

"The stuff of nightmares," Fay whispered, fear swinging in her voice.

"Get behind me," I commanded and tightened the grip on my axe.

The beast roared again, saliva dripping from its three rows of razor-sharp teeth, and in the distance, two others answered. I wasn't sure I could handle one of them. I most definitely couldn't fight three. This monster was in an entirely different league from the rakefangs or even most of the other predators I'd watched in the Trials. Fay was right. It was the stuff of nightmares indeed, bred for fear and death.

The legs were covered in thick plates that didn't look as if my axe would even make a dent into. My mate stood no chance against it with her wooden spear. But we would fight.

Fight until the end.

"I will find you again," I promised Fay. "If we don't end up together in the afterlife, I will find you. I promise."

She didn't reply, but I felt her trepidation through our bond. She was scared, although she didn't show it. A lesser female would have trembled, cried, screamed. Not my mate.

I growled at the beast, exposing my tusks. Every muscle was tense, ready for the battle. But the beast didn't attack. It was waiting for something. The other two monsters? Once they arrived, we didn't even stand the hint of a chance.

So I attacked.

I launched myself into the air, flying in a wide arch, my axe ready to drink the blood of my enemies. I gave myself to the feral beast within me, letting go of all civilised thought. I unleashed myself upon the beast and when I landed right in front of it, my axe struck true. It sliced into the closest leg, right where the plates met, where I'd hoped it would be the most vulnerable. Bright yellow blood spluttered all over me. The beast screamed, so loud that I wanted to cover my ears. Yet I'd only injured the leg, not severed it. The monster kicked at me, moving faster than its huge stature should allow. I evaded it by throwing myself to the left. I rolled, jumped to my feet, sliced at another leg, but the beast moved before the axe could hit the weakest spot. Harmlessly, my blade glided over the plates. The momentum unbalanced me just enough. When the monster kicked out again, I wasn't able to evade it.

Agony shattered through me when its claw raked over my shoulder. My right arm went limp; it must have severed something important. I dimly heard Fay scream, but I couldn't turn to look at her. I had to continue fighting before the beast could decide that my mate was more interesting than me.

The axe seemed heavier than before. My vision swam. I could feel the blood pouring out of me and with it, my life force.

Fay needed me.

Gathering all the strength I had left, I swung my axe. It bit through the last remnants holding the beast's leg together. The lower part of the leg fell to the ground, yellow blood leaking from it. The beast roared in anger. I evaded it again, and again, but I was on the defensive now and my energy was fading fast. I wouldn't be able to fight it much longer, let alone go back on the offensive.

Fay needed me. I had to protect my mate.

Something struck my head from behind. The world flickered. My legs buckled, but I barely felt my knees hitting the ground.

A huge claw pressed against my chest, pinning me down. Saliva dripped onto me as the beast lowered its gaping maw.

Everything was fading. If I was lucky, I'd be unconscious before those teeth could tear into my flesh. I let my head roll to the side.

My mate, facing three deadly monsters with only a wooden stick, was the last thing I saw before darkness claimed me.

19

FAY

I cursed the mating bond as I sank to my feet, Vruhag's pain too much to bear. When the horrible spider-alien had raked its claw over the orc's shoulder, it had felt as if I had been attacked myself. Despite the agony, Vruhag continued fighting, but I could feel that he was getting weaker. There was nothing I could do. I had a spear, but I had no idea what to actually do with it. If an axe couldn't hurt the huge spider, then my spear would do as much damage as a toothpick. Still, I clutched it tightly, my only weapon against the monster. If Vruhag fell, I might get in one good stab before the alien killed me.

It was only a matter of time. The orc was unsteady on his feet, his lunges no longer elegant. He managed to evade the spider most of the time, but he was tiring fast. Blood was streaming down his chest, soaking his kilt. It was a miracle he was still standing.

But then he fell. The spider pinned him down with

one disgusting leg, then lowered its head. It was going to eat my mate.

My heart shattered into pieces. In this very moment, I knew that he'd been right, that he really was my mate. And I regretted resisting. Regretted not kissing him earlier. Regretted every harsh word I'd said, every moment I hadn't spent in his arms, because now it was too late.

The spider monster opened its huge jaws. Rows of sharp teeth glittered menacingly.

There was no way I would just stand and watch. A scream burst from my lips, a warrior's cry, and I lifted my spear and-

A blindingly bright light drowned out the world. I squeezed my eyes shut but continued holding the spear in front of me, just in case the spider could see despite the brightness. It felt as if I was lifted into the air, but then my feet hit solid ground again just a heartbeat later. Maybe I'd imagined it. What was this? Some new torture by the game makers?

"Stop waving that spear or you'll hurt someone."

A woman's voice. And she was speaking English.

I froze, blinking into the bright light, desperate to see what was going on.

"Decontamination complete," came a computer's toneless voice, and the light switched off.

I was no longer in the forest. I was on a spaceship. It was nothing like the cell I'd been imprisoned on before they'd flown me down to the planet. No, this was a welcoming place full of warmth and colour. I stood in what seemed like a futuristic living room with floating sofas that had seen better days and a table covered in clutter. And in front of me, a woman, a human woman.

Blue eyes sparkled beneath a mop of curly blonde hair. She was younger and a few inches shorter than me, but her confident presence more than made up for it. Her tight grey tank top highlighted her lean build and muscular arms. She either worked out regularly or had a physically demanding job. Or regularly fought monsters on Kalumbu.

"Hi, I'm Penny," she said cheerfully. "Welcome to the Artep."

"Hi," I stammered. "Where am I?"

The oldest question in the book. I felt a little silly asking it.

"We're on a spaceship currently in orbit around Kalumbu. We beamed you up and just in time, me thinks. You can drop the spear now. You're safe here."

I realised I was still clutching my weapon, the tip pointing at Penny's chest. I lowered it, but didn't let go. This seemed too good to be true. What were the chances of being rescued by a fellow human? It had to be a trick. Maybe the spider had poisoned me with a hallucinogenic.

"Where's Vruhag?" I demanded, my voice shaking only a tiny bit.

"The green alien? He's in the med bay, we beamed him right into a med pod. He's getting fixed as we speak, don't worry."

"I want to see him."

The woman smiled at me. "You will, later. Right now we'd only get in the way. Besides, you're the first human I've seen in over two years. I need some girl time."

I gaped at her. "Two years?"

"Long story. Let's sit, you look like you could do with a drink. Petra, make us two of those bubbly cocktails."

"Petra?"

"The ship's computer. Whatever you need, just ask her and she'll provide it. More or less. I've been trying to teach her to make margaritas but no luck so far."

Penny sat down on one of the floating couches and patted the soft blue fabric on her right.

Instead of joining her, I took a seat opposite. I leaned the spear against the sofa, close enough to reach in an emergency.

The other woman shrugged. "I get it. You've been through a lot. We watched it all. Well, the beginning, then you disappeared somehow. The next time we saw you, you were in a different place with that green guy of yours. What is he, come to think of it?"

"He calls himself an orc. His name is Vruhag."

Penny grinned. "He's very handsome. Good for you, girl. What does he smell like?"

I thought I'd misheard her for a moment. "Smell?"

"My mate, Qong, smells like waffles. It's how I found him. Smelled waffles on the space station I was working on, followed the scent, found my mate. That's the short version, anyway. They say that in some cases, the bond will make your mate smell like your favourite food."

I remembered trying to pin down Vruhag's scent. Cinnamon with pepper and fresh grass. Honey and milk and cardamom. Earth after rain. I'd been unable to define it. Would it be different now, after I'd accepted him? He didn't even know. Didn't realise that I'd regretted not giving into the bond sooner. I had to tell him.

I got to my feet at the same time as a tray floated into the room.

"Ah, our drinks. Thanks, Petra."

"You are welcome," said the same disembodied voice that I'd heard when I'd arrived. "Would you like any snacks?"

Penny took two crystal glasses from the tray and handed me one. "That would be lovely. Only human-grade food. Don't sneak in Mondian treats again just because you want to impress the Captain."

She sat down again and waited for me to do the same.

"Relax, your mate is fine," she said reassuringly. "If your bond is anything like mine, you'd know if he was in pain, right?"

I nodded slowly. She was right. I'd feel if he was unwell. Right now, all I could sense through the bond was a peaceful calm. He was likely unconscious, but at least he wasn't in pain any longer.

I sat down again, clutching the glass. "How did you rescue us? This is a rescue, right? You're not going to hand us to the game makers or sell us as...slaves?"

Penny's expression turned cold. "I was a slave for two years. I was abducted from Earth and forced to clean the sewers of a space station. The job nobody else would do. Trust me, I would never, ever do that to anyone. Least of all a fellow human."

"Sorry," I muttered.

"Don't worry about it. After what you've been through, I understand that you can't just trust me. I've had two years to come to terms with it all. How long were you at the station before entering the Trials?"

"I don't know. I woke up in a dark cell and was in there for maybe a few hours before..."

"Kalumbu," Penny said with a nod. "It's an awful place. Qong and I had just escaped the station ourselves and were getting settled here on the Artep when we saw the broadcast. I couldn't believe it. I'd thought I'd never see another human again, yet there you were. There was no way we could leave after that. So I persuaded Twim - that's the captain of this ship - to rescue you."

She took a sip of her drink and sighed in contentment. "This stuff is good. Try it. Anyway, turns out you can't just beam someone off Kalumbu. There are all sorts of security measures in place. Silus, one of Twim's guys, hacked their system for long enough to get you out, but it was a close call."

I made a mental note to thank the captain and his crew.

"What happens now?" I asked. "Is there a way back to Earth?"

"I don't know. Maybe. We're a long way from home. You'd have to find a way to pay for the journey. Or your mate, if he has the cash. But do you really want to go back? After finding your mate?"

"Yes," I said automatically. Ever since I'd realised I was no longer on Earth, I'd wanted to return. It had been all I could think about. But Vruhag... he couldn't come with me. I didn't know what would happen to him, but it would probably involve scientists and dissections. He was too different, too *alien*. Not something that could be explained as a costume or mask. I had to think about it all. Later. Once I knew he was alright, once I had a quiet moment to process everything.

"'Twim might know how to get there," Penny said with a small smile. "He's a grumpy old git, but his heart is in its right place. Just don't let him realise that you know. He likes to pretend that he's a tough outlaw."

"I *am* a tough outlaw."

I jumped to my feet, my glass shattering on the floor. Cold liquid covered my bare feet.

He looked like a werewolf, covered head to toe in golden fur that was turning grey in places. His tail was casually wrapped around one furry leg, while long claws sprouted from his fingers. His yellow eyes bored into me as if he was trying to read my soul.

"May I introduce the captain, Twim," Penny said calmly. "'Twim, this is Fay."

"Welcome to the Artep," he said in his deep, husky

voice. His whiskers quivered with amusement at a joke I didn't understand. "And please don't listen to anything this Peritan says. I am a tough, experienced captain who likes to drink the blood of his enemies. At least that's what I let everyone believe."

He grinned, exposing sharp canines. He was handsome in a rugged, feral sort of way. But nowhere near as attractive as Vruhag, of course. After him, I didn't think I could find any guy, human or alien, as alluring as my mate.

"I'm about to check on our other new passenger," the captain continued. "Would you like to join me?"

I nodded, then remembered that he might misinterpret that. "Yes. How can I understand you, by the way? Are you speaking English?"

Twim laughed. "The Artep is translating for us until we can fit you with an implant."

"The ship is translating? But I hear you as if you were speaking my language."

"Look at my lips. You'll notice my mouth movements don't match the words you hear. The Artep translates neurally, broadcasting right into your mind. It doesn't work for all species, but my ship has been able to practice on Penny." He shot a look at the other woman, who rolled her eyes in response.

"Only because my brain slug has been malfunctioning. I think it's not happy about my new surroundings. Specifically the captain."

Twim grinned wolfishly. "If you don't like it here, maybe you'd like to go for a space walk?"

As much as I enjoyed their easy banter, I wanted to see my mate. I grabbed my spear - you could never be careful enough - and turned to one of the two doors. "I'm ready."

"Good. But it's this way," Twim said drily and led me out of the other door.

"Do you want me to come with you?" Penny asked.

I shook my head. As nice as it was to have someone who understood what I was going through, I wanted time alone with Vruhag. I had so much to say to him. I almost hoped that he would stay unconscious so I could tell him everything without the fear of how he'd react. Talking to someone was so much easier while they couldn't hear your words.

I followed Twim through the spaceship, trying to take in everything while also feeling very lost and very overwhelmed. I was on a spaceship. That sentence itself boggled my mind. Yes, I'd been on an alien planet and before that, a space station, but... it wasn't the same. This vessel could fly through space. Could reach places I didn't even know existed.

The ship was clean, but clearly not new. Some of the walls had metal patches, while occasionally we'd walk past loose cables and flickering lights.

"Just through here," the captain said before we passed through a wide doorway. "Your mate is in the pod on the right."

I hurried over to the silver cocoon that he was pointing to. The top half was translucent, giving me a view of a sleeping Vruhag. Dried blood still caked his green skin, but the wound on his shoulder had disappeared. As had many of the other scars and barely healed wounds that had previously marred his body.

"Why is he still unconscious?" I asked.

"He's in an induced healing sleep," someone replied. I turned to see a living plant. I tried to keep my expression neutral, but it was hard. While Twim and Vruhag were humanoid, this alien was very much the opposite. If she hadn't just spoken, I would have thought she was, well, a giant plant. A bulbous body that resembled a huge radish stood on thick tendrils, dozens of them. Her eyes and mouth were at the top of the body, without a separate head. And instead of arms, more tendrils grew from her sides, each at least two metres long.

"Meet Zee, our medical officer," Twim introduced her. "They've been looking after your mate."

"Vruhag," I corrected. I didn't like how they kept referring to him as my mate instead of using his name. Yes, I'd realised that there was a bond between us, but that didn't mean we'd stopped being individuals. I didn't want anyone to see me simply as Vruhag's mate. Although I suspected that the orc in question would be very happy to hear me referred to as such.

"He's strong," Zee said, tendrils wriggling. "I can wake him now, but I wanted to wait until you're here. We watched the Trials and it seemed as if your bond isn't complete yet. Is that correct?"

"We didn't get the chance."

"When he wakes up, his mating fever will know no

bounds. He will lack the strength to control it. Are you ready to deal with that or do you want us to restrain him?"

I looked down at him, sleeping so peacefully. I'd never seen him this relaxed. The smallest of smiles curved his lips, as if he was having a pleasant dream. I wanted to touch him, run my fingers through his long hair, rub my thumb over his lips, the lips that had felt so amazing when we'd kissed. We'd thought it was our last chance. A first and final kiss before we died. Now everything had changed. We were safe. I breathed in deep. Safe. I still couldn't believe it. Didn't want to believe it just in case it was all a trap. A game.

Yet my instincts told me that it was real. We really had been rescued. We were safe. And that meant, we had a future.

I turned to Zee. "I'm ready. But there are one or two things I need."

20
VRUHAG

Everything around me was quiet. I kept my eyes closed and took in my surroundings, pretending to be still asleep. I couldn't hear nor smell the monster anymore. But the fresh scent of the forest was also missing, just an echo of it clinging to my skin. We were no longer in the jungle. And that slight whirr, the vibration against my back so faint most people would have ignored it, signalled that I was on a spaceship or station.

Horror roiled through me. They'd taken me back to my cell. Taken my mate from me.

My diamond claws pushed through my skin, but I stayed still for now. I'd have to gather more information. Turning into a raging berserker wouldn't bring my mate back.

I could still smell her. She was close. At least they hadn't left her on Kalumbu to be killed and eaten by those monsters. But why had they taken us back to the station? The show's viewers would be disappointed. They didn't get to see the bloody deaths they desired.

Unless... no, Fay was alive, I felt it through our bond. I concentrated on that invisible band connecting our souls. She was...happy. Relieved. And slightly apprehensive.

Not emotions I'd expect her to experience while prisoner of the game makers. So why was she happy? What had happened?

Footsteps outside the cell. I took a few deep breaths, then opened my eyes.

This wasn't a cell, wasn't the space station.

I was on a large bed, big enough for an orc and his mate, in a room barely big enough for it. Only a small gap between the bed and the wall led to a door. There was no other furniture. Not even a shelf. Just a room with a bed. On one wall, a screen offered a source of information, but it was switched off.

Where was I?

The footsteps halted outside the door. And her scent overwhelmed me.

Fay. My mate.

I sat up, amazed that I felt no pain. Not even a twinge in my muscles. I dared throw a glance at my shoulder where the eight-legged monster had cut me. Nothing. My skin was smooth without any trace of injury or scar. Only an advanced med pod could do that. I doubted the game makers would heal me just so they could take me back to Kalumbu.

Fay's happiness glimmered through our bond.

That left only one option. This was the afterlife. We'd perished on Kalumbu, but had found each other again after death, just as I had hoped.

I smiled. Eternity to spend with my mate. I was looking forward to every click.

I sheathed my diamond claws again, convinced that we were no longer in danger. What a strange feeling. Safe. We'd made it out of Kalumbu. Not alive, but at least we were together. I didn't know why the afterlife looked like a spaceship, but I didn't care.

"Are you awake?" Fay asked through the closed door.

She'd already know, feel it through our bond.

"I am."

The door slid open with a whine that spoke of unoiled mechanisms. The gods of the afterlife clearly didn't look after this place very well.

I got up, not wanting to appear weak by sitting on the bed.

And there she was, wrapped in a silky red robe that hugged her tiny figure. Her mane pooled onto her shoulders, sleek and freshly brushed. Her lips were covered in some sort of paint that made me want to lick it off. Her scent enveloped me, stronger than ever, sweet as nectar, spicy as sin. She was aroused.

I looked down at myself. I was naked, the kilt gone. My shaft had pushed through its protective casing, fully visible and erect. Ready for my mate.

The urge to claim her rushed through my body,

incensing every cell. Rational thought was swept from my mind as the mating fever took over.

"Mate," I growled and prowled towards her.

She smiled at me, happiness and contentment radiating from her. The door slid closed behind her, the final signal that now was time to let go.

"I can't hold back," I breathed.

She looked at me, her eyes swirling with emotion. Then she let the robe drop to the floor.

"Then don't," Fay whispered.

She was achingly beautiful. I thought she'd looked alluring in that woven dress that left little to the imagination, but it had only been a single petal of the flower that she was. When I'd first looked at her, back in my cell, I'd only seen her weaknesses, the lack of scales and claws. Now, I saw the strength in her. Felt it as she looked at me with confidence. She wasn't afraid to show herself to me. She bared it all. Offered herself to me, her mate.

"Claim me," she said, her voice husky. "I want to be your mate."

The words echoed through my heart, my soul.

And I snapped.

I pounced, grabbed her as gently as I could despite the roaring in my ears, and threw her onto the bed. I spread her legs, dropped to my knees, and stared at that mound between her thighs, the sweet-smelling haven that was calling to me, begging to be worshipped.

She didn't look like an orc female. There was no skin flap to hide her mating tube that I'd have to carefully pry open. Yet Fay was perfect for me. I knew we were compatible because we were mates. There was no doubt in the mind that when it came to claiming her, I'd fit.

Pushing her legs apart even further, I took in the glistening wetness before I could no longer hold back. I buried my head between her thighs and ran my tongue along her slit, lapping up that wetness like an animal. Her taste exploded in my mouth, the most delicious nectar I'd ever tasted. I licked her again, and she moaned softly. Her hands settled on my head, her fingers tangling my mane. She held me in place, guiding me to where she wanted me.

I was a fast learner. Her moans and swallowed cries grew louder every time my tongue swirled around that little knob, a spot of pleasure that I couldn't get enough of. Neither could Fay. She writhed against me, her thighs locked around me. I loved how she showed me the way to giving her satisfaction. I wanted her to feel the same fire burning through my veins.

All I could think about was Fay. The world had ceased to exist around us. My mate, pleasuring her, worshipping her, was all that mattered.

I sucked on the knob, gave it a lick, sucked it again, and Fay exploded. She screamed, her hands clawed at me, wetness gushed out of her where I was waiting, ready to lap it all up. She quivered, her legs shaking. Through our bond, I could feel her ecstasy and it made me almost spill myself onto the bed.

I stopped licking her, giving her a moment to recover, but she tore at my mane, gasping for more.

So I complied. I slowed my pace a little but kept exploring, experimenting, testing her limits.

My shaft was harder than ever before. I needed to claim her soon, but was she ready? She was so small. I didn't want to hurt her. Mating fever be damned. I could never forgive myself if I injured her during the claiming.

I licked my index finger, making sure it was wet all over, then gently pushed it into her tight channel. She clenched around my finger, her inner muscles trying to hold me in place. My mate was as possessive as me. I loved her for it.

I pushed in as far as I could. My finger didn't reach the bottom of her cave, giving me hope that my shaft would fit.

Carefully, I added a second finger. Fay moaned, arching her back, pushing her hips towards me. She wanted more. Needed more.

She was so tight around me, but wet enough to let me slide in and out. I pushed my fingers apart ever so slightly, testing how much I could stretch her. Fay gasped in response, but it was from pleasure, not pain.

"Fuck me," she groaned breathessly.

I didn't need her to say it twice. I pulled out my fingers, licked her precious nectar off them, before positioning myself between her legs. My shaft was pulsing, the tip leaking the first drop of my seed. The lower wings were still wrapped around my shaft, but they were loosening, getting ready to expand once I was embedded deep within my mate.

I leaned over my mate so that I could see her face. Her cheeks were flushed with pink, her pupils dilated, her lips parted. I couldn't resist kissing her. Just a moment's delay. Her lips met mine, soft and demanding. Her tongue pushed against mine, something I'd never even considered doing during a kiss, but maybe it was something she expected from a male. So I returned the favour, exploring her mouth with my tongue, dancing with hers. A deep growl grew in my chest. This was what I'd been looking for all my life. And now I was home.

With one last playful swipe of my tongue, I ended the kiss.

Fay's wide eyes met mine. I looked into her soul and opened my heart to her. I wouldn't hold back anything. She was part of me now, the most precious part of me. I'd never let her go.

I reached between us and held my shaft against her entrance, never breaking eye contact with my mate.

And in my mind, I heard her voice.

Mine.

21

FAY

I didn't know sex could be like this. The things he'd done to me, how he'd licked me, made me shatter...

And he was only just beginning. Vruhag's dark eyes bored into me, making sure I was ready for him.

When I'd entered the room, I'd got a glimpse of his cock. The shape wasn't all that different from what I was used to, but the size... I didn't quite know yet how he could possibly fit.

At the base of his cock had been a strange fold of skin, but I'd not got a chance to take a closer look. Yet. And beneath, three huge balls had hung like thick sacks, the same dark green as his cock. For a moment, I wondered what colour his cum would be. Not that it mattered. It didn't matter that Vruhag was green, that he had tusks, that his ears were long, that his fingernails could turn into claws.

All that mattered was that he was my mate.

His cock pushed against my entrance. I spread my

thighs further to make it easier for him. And still he wasn't taking his eyes off me. He was fucking me with his heated gaze, preparing me for what was to come. I was melting under those dark eyes of his, turning into a moaning, writhing addict. Addicted to the pleasure he could give me. Addicted to his scent that filled the room. Addicted to the feel of his tongue against my folds.

I looked up at him and knew that he was my mate.

Mine, I said to him, not bothering to move my lips.

He grinned, tusks flashing, and growled, "Mine."

And then he pushed in. Drove his cock so deep that tears sprang to my eyes. It hurt, so tight, so full, but it was a good pain. I was glad he hadn't gone slow. I needed this. Needed him inside me, proof that he was real, that *this* was real.

Looking deep into his eyes, I watched as the last scrap of control fled him. His gaze turned feral. And he fucked me. There was no other word for it.

He roared like a beast as his cock pummelled in and out of me, fucking me senseless. I clawed at the sheets, looking for something to hold on. His balls slapped against my arse, so hard that the sound echoed through the room, mixing with the grunts and roars of the orc.

He moved so fast, in and out, almost leaving my aching pussy before pushing in all the way to the limit.

I loved it. Every second of it. The pain, the stretching, the slapping of his balls.

His eyes had turned savage. He was lost in the rutting as he claimed me.

I tried to squeeze my inner walls around him, wanted to be more of a part of this wild fuck, but he was too big.

Together, we hurtled towards oblivion, gasping, screaming, crying out for more.

Again and again, he growled my name. And I moaned his every time he hit that spot deep within me, driving me further into madness.

Just before the edge of the cliff, I reached up, got hold of his hair and pulled him down. I wanted to taste him when I exploded around him.

But I should have known better. He was an orc. He flashed me a grin and before I knew what was happening, his mouth was against the nape of my neck, his tusks digging into my skin.

With one last forceful push, he drove us to the edge.

And then he bit me.

I exploded. Shattered. Erupted. And he was with me, holding me together while pushing me further than I'd ever gone before. The pain was a distant memory as we floated together, our souls dancing with joy.

We were mates. We had claimed each other. And the stars were sparkling with approval.

I don't know how long we drifted, riding the wave that took us beyond our mortal bodies. From a distance, I felt something expand within me. Not where the thick crown of his cock still stretched me, but closer to my entrance. It felt good. That was all that mattered.

I fell asleep at some point, curled up on his chest after he'd rolled us over. His strong arms were wrapped protectively around us. After the horrors of Kalumbu, I needed this. Had to know that I was safe, that no one could hurt us. Safe.

I woke up when something moved between my legs. I yawned, completely relaxed. I was still on top of Vruhag. His eyes were closed and there was a contented smile on his face. So different from the orc I'd seen launching himself at that spider-monster. He'd been feral then. And feral again when he'd fucked me. There were two sides to him. One battle-hardened, alien and primitive, the other kind, caring and gentle.

He was perfect. Vruhag was the best mate any woman could imagine. And he was mine. At some point, I'd have to think about what our future together would look like, but not now. I just wanted to enjoy the moment.

A pressure I had no longer noticed lessened. With a squelching sound, Vruhag's cock slipped out of me.

Had he been inside me this entire time, while we'd slept? How was that even possible?

We should probably have a shower. The cabin the captain had assigned us didn't have its own bathroom, but the communal cleaning room, as the aliens called it, was just two doors down the corridor. And it was big enough for both of us. I licked my lips as I imagined what showering together might lead to.

I shouldn't. We'd had the best sex of my life, I'd had two mind-blowing orgasms, and I should really focus on other things now. But that was impossible while I was in Vruhag's arms, hearing his heart beat, smelling his alluring scent that made me horny all over again.

"The wings have folded," Vruhag muttered sleepily.

"Huh?"

"My wings. They kept me locked inside you until now."

I was too curious to stay where I was. I rolled onto the mattress, ignoring the sticky wetness between my legs - I really needed a shower - and took a proper look at Vruhag's cock. He was half-erect, making me wonder how on Earth he'd fit inside me. At the base, the skin folds I'd dimly noticed last night were now expanded, looking a bit like, well, like wings. I imagined them plugging my entrance while his cock was still in me, preventing him from slipping out. And keeping his cum in.

"Contraception," I blurted. "I don't have any."

Vruhag lazily blinked at me. "We're dead. There is no need."

And that's how we spent half an hour arguing, me telling him that we were very much alive, him convinced that we were in the afterlife, until I gave up.

If I hadn't been naked, I'd simply have dragged him

outside until he met one of the crew, or Penny and her mate. But while my robe was somewhere on the floor, Vruhag had been carried here as naked as the day he was born. Assuming that he had been *born* and not hatched from an egg or something.

"Petra, tell this oaf that we're alive."

The screen on the wall opposite flashed to life, showing two heartbeat graphs.

"I can confirm that you are showing signs of life," the ship's computer replied. "Do you want me to start a full medical diagnosis?"

I laughed. "Unnecessary. Do you believe me now?"

"But...how?" Vruhag looked around the room, looked at me as if he was seeing everything with new eyes.

"It's a long story and I don't have all the details yet myself, but there's another human here on the ship, a woman named Penny. She and her mate escaped from the space station where the two of us were held. When they were on this ship, they saw a broadcast of the Trials. Penny persuaded the Artep's captain to rescue us."

Vruhag gaped at me. "That's impossible. Kalumbu is shielded, nobody should be able to get through their security."

"Penny mentioned one of the aliens hacked their systems. Don't ask me how they pulled it off, but I can reassure you that we're not dead. And now we're free."

I could feel his trepidation through our bond. He

still wasn't letting himself believe me. He was scared that it was all yet another trick by the game makers.

I took his hands, squeezing them reassuringly. Without his diamond claws out, they weren't all that different from human hands. If you ignored the green calluses and that there were only four fingers instead of five.

"We're free," I repeated. "We're safe."

Finally, his eyes lit up with undiluted joy. "We're safe." He pulled me against his chest again and squeezed me tightly. I let him. And when he started massaging one of my breasts, I also let him do that.

We didn't leave the bed for another day, until we had explored each other's bodies and fucked and slept and eaten and laughed together.

If only life could have stayed that way.

22
VRUHAG

The ship's entire crew had assembled on their spacious bridge, along with the Peritan female, Penny, and her Gofren mate, Qong. The scaled male was intimidating at first glance, but he had a wicked sense of humour that immediately made me like him. As long as he kept far away from my mate.

I stood between her and everyone else, unwilling to let her anywhere near another male. The aftereffect of the mating fever had me on edge. She'd been unwilling to stay away from the ship's males until I'd told her that right now, I wasn't sure if I could stop myself from killing them if they as much as touched her. Only when I'd reassured Fay that this wasn't me, that I wasn't someone who would never let her speak to another male, did she back down. I hoped the mating fever would disappear quickly. I'd claimed her so often that it should be satisfied by now.

My shaft hardened at the thought of how I'd taken

her in the shower. She'd been on all fours while I'd claimed her from behind. The water had fallen on us like warm rain, muffling out our groans. We'd cleaned each other, which had resulted in another round of passionate mating. Every time I'd thought I was sated, she'd looked at me with those gorgeous eyes and my shaft rose into action once more.

"Focus," Fay whispered, clearly feeling my arousal through our bond.

I gave her a lopsided grin. She knew what awaited her as soon as this meeting was over. My sire had spent two weeks locked into his home after he'd met my ama. I'd been told the stories growing up, his legendary prowess and stamina. I could easily see me outlasting him. Every time I looked at my mate, I was hard once again. It was never enough, the hunger for her never quite sated. I tried to go slow, give her breaks, but it was so hard to control those urges.

"If you've not met our latest two passengers yet," Captain Twim began, "say hello to Fay and her mate, Vruhag. I know some of you may be a little wary of having an orc on board the Artep, but Vruhag has reassured me that he's from one of the civilised clans of Orcadia."

Fay snickered softly. I gave her a hard look, promising to show her just how civilised I could be.

The captain turned to us. "Have you decided what you want to do? We can drop you off at a planet or station en route, for a price of course, but we always have room for a warrior on our crew. Especially one who has survived the Trials."

"We have not had time to talk about it," I said and was rewarded with knowing laughter from the crew. "But I thank you for the offer. I want to thank you all for rescuing us from Kalumbu. We are in your debt."

"We may be outlaws, but that doesn't mean we don't have morals," Twim replied gravely. "When Penny told us that you had not entered the Trials by choice and that Peritans come from a protected planet, we had to intervene. I always assumed that warriors entered the Trials for money and glory, but it seems that is not the truth."

"I have a ship, the Bloodstar. They took me from it. Can you scan for it? All my belongings are on there, including my savings. I would like to pay you for rescuing us."

Admitting that they'd indeed saved us left a bitter taste in my mouth. I wasn't used to needing someone to rescue me. I was an orc, a warrior, and I hoped none of my kin would ever find out what had happened.

Twim nodded at a male sitting at one of the bridge consoles. I'd never seen his species before. His upper body looked strangely similar to Peritans, but his lower half was that of a beast, with furry legs and hooves rather than feet. Huge horns curled around the sides of his head. Many species with horns had a direct correlation between the size of their adornments and the size of their mating shafts. I growled before I could stop myself.

"This is Silus. He's the one who hacked the security systems surrounding Kalumbu. He might be able to find your ship."

The male gave me a confirming glance, but didn't smile. He looked grim, angry almost.

"I will help, but I have something to share with you all first. "We have a problem." Silus typed something and a mess of alien writing appeared on the main screen. "When I hacked the station, I had some bots copy as much data as possible. I was planning to sell whatever they found, but luckily, I had a quick look first. Check out this list."

"What is it?" Twim asked.

"It lists all the future contestants they currently house on the station. And look here, where it states their species. These two females aren't the only Peritans. There are more."

Penny gasped while Fay made a choking sound behind me. I immediately wrapped my arms around her, shielding her from the world. She leaned her head against my chest and I could feel her sadness and worry pulsate through our bond.

"How many?" I asked, my word sharp enough to cut through steel.

"I can see two more on this manifest, but that doesn't mean there aren't others. My bots didn't look for anything specific, so there may be more data they didn't copy."

"What do the other things on the screen mean?" Penny asked, her voice quaking with anger.

"It's the length of time the contestants have been in cryosleep."

"Cryosleep," Fay echoed. "So they're asleep? They're not suffering?"

Her anger was making me see green. I wanted to hit something, make someone bleed. They'd taken three Peritan females and taken them to a hellhole far from their planet, only to make them suffer and die. It was monstrous.

"I need some more time to study the data," Silus said gently, "but I think you should know the truth."

He looked straight at me and I realised he was trying to see Fay, hidden in my embrace. Slowly, I let go of her and let her turn to face the hacker, but I kept my hands on her hips, steadying her for whatever other revelations he was about to spill.

"Fay, you were brought to the station at the same time as the other females. You were in cryosleep as well."

"How long?" Fay asked tonelessly.

I tightened my grip on her, fearing the answer.

"According to the computer, it converts to seventy Peritan years."

I didn't know how much that was in IG years, but Fay's reaction told me everything I needed to know. She became very still, very quiet, shutting out the world. She didn't cry or scream, but through our bond, I felt her anguish.

Seventy years. That means they're all gone. My friends. My family.

Ignoring the others, I lifted her into my arms and carried her to our cabin. She didn't move until the doors closed behind us. Only then did she let the tears flow freely.

Fay's grief turned into anger, then into hunger for action. She prowled the Artep's corridors like a warrior looking for battle.

To my relief, nobody questioned the need to rescue those other Peritans. I didn't know who Twim and his crew were, what they'd done to become outlaws, but the captain had been truthful when he'd said that they had morals. All of them had a sense of justice that matched my own. It was wrong to send unarmed females into the Trials. They wouldn't be as lucky as us. At least Fay and I had had each other. And the chii.

I wondered how our little friends were doing. One of the crew was always watching the Trials, keeping an eye out for the chii and any mention of how we'd escaped. But the Trials continued as if nothing happened. The game makers had given an official statement saying that we'd been killed by monsters before their cameras could get to us. But I knew they'd seen how we'd been beamed off Kalumbu. Knew they'd be searching for us. We knew too much. If we told the world that the contestants weren't there by their own free choice, it would impact their viewing figures. Sponsors might decide that was one step too far. In a way, we now held power over the game makers, but I doubted they saw it that way.

We still weren't safe.

Not that I told Fay of my worries. She had enough on her mind. I was glad she had Penny. The two females were quickly becoming friends, their shared trauma bringing them closer. But at night, Fay was mine. Sometimes, I was slow and gentle, showing her just how much I loved her. Other times, she begged me to let go of all inhibitions, even if that meant leaving bruises. She loved it when I bit her. Went crazy for it. And one night, she bit me, staking her claim.

I couldn't have been any prouder of my mate.

Despite the troubles, the worries, I was sure we had a future together. We'd rescue the Peritans, make the game makers pay, and then we'd leave the Artep, make a life for ourselves somewhere else. Maybe that would be Orcadia. Maybe we'd travel the universe in the Bloodstar. Maybe we'd visit Peritus and see how it had changed since Fay had been abducted.

We had so many options. Because finally, we were free.

"Penny for your thoughts?" Fay whispered into my ear, her hot breath tickling my skin.

"What does Penny have to do with anything?"

My mate laughed. "Not Penny. A penny. An old Earth currency. Forget it. I was asking what you're thinking about. Your face looked all grave and gloomy, but then you smiled."

"Hope," I said simply. "I have hope. We're going to have a wonderful life, you and I. Once all this is over."

"Once all this is over," Fay confirmed. "Where shall we go? Is there somewhere you've always wanted to visit?"

I thought for a moment. "Epsyl-4. The mountains there are made of diamonds. I'd like to cut off a tiny piece and make it into a necklace for you."

Again, she laughed. "That's so very you. Cut off a piece of a mountain."

"Why not? The mountains won't miss it. And you are worthy of being clad in diamonds from top to bottom. But we shall start with a necklace and work our way up from there."

"Epsyl-4," she said, tasting the name. "Why not."

"And on the way, we will stop at the Great Library Station. I promised I'd take you there, remember?"

Her eyes lit up. "I didn't think you'd remember."

I cupped her cheeks. "I remember every moment. Every single moment since I first smelled your scent. Every heartbeat is ingrained in my memory. And I will treasure every memory, the good and the bad, because it all led to this. To our future."

I pulled her close until our lips met. We kissed, sealing our future, a life filled with love and hope.

We were free.

If you don't want a cliffhanger, stop here and continue

reading in My Big Furry Alien Satyr, *book two of this series. Otherwise, continue for a sneak peek of Silus' story.*

Want to find out how Penny and Qong met? Read My Big Sweet Waffle Monster *for free by signing up to my newsletter:*
https://skyemackinnon.com/wafflemonster

If you enjoyed this book, please take a moment to leave a review.

EPILOGUE

SILUS

It was my turn to watch the Trials. I hated every moment of sitting in my cabin, staring at the screen, watching as contestants were torn apart by beasts or by each other. We were taking turns to avoid becoming desensitised to the violence. None of us were good people. We'd done bad things. Committed crimes. There was a reason why we were in this part of the galaxy, where outlaws were the norm and the Intergalactic Authority had little power. But I had rules; I had limits. There were some things I wouldn't do. I'd not lost my soul quite yet. Stained it, tarnished it, yes, but it was still there. Tattered and curled up in the darkness of all the things I'd done.

Before all this, I'd never watched the Trials. I'd known how to access them, of course, but I'd always had a bad feeling about them. Watching contestants fight to the death, perish in the harsh jungles of Kalumbu, eaten alive by beasts bred to be always hungry - it wasn't for me.

I clenched my teeth and chose the Trials channel. It was on a hidden frequency that could only be accessed by those who knew what they were doing. A new episode had just begun. The Trials were streaming all day, every day, but some of it were repeats, showing the bloodiest battles and the most horrific deaths in a loop. We weren't interested in those. It gave us some breaks in between watching the Trials, and it meant every crew member only had to spend an IG hour a day in front of our screens.

I should have brought snacks, but yesterday's episode had turned my stomach. I wondered if any of the contestants had volunteered to take part or if they were all victims, abducted from their homes or spaceships and forced to fight for the entertainment of others. I wished we could rescue them all. Destroy the Trials once and for all. But that was too dangerous. There was a multi-trillion industry behind the Trials of Kalumbu. Powerful people watched the games, sponsored contestants, bet on them. We'd become even bigger targets if we ended the games. Rescuing a few contestants would hopefully be enough to make a difference without turning ourselves into martyrs.

The first two contestants presented to the audience were males, one Pletorian and one battle-scarred Kardarian, but the third made me clutch my horns. A female and a Peritan at that.

Breathless, I watched as she blinked into the camera, blinded by the bright lights around her. She was naked, vulnerable, and shivering with fear. I touched the screen before I realised what I was doing. The image froze right at the moment the camera had zoomed in, focusing on the female's face.

Her skin was the colour of my fur, exactly the same shades of brown. Her eyes were a warm amber, framed by long lashes. Her hair had been shaved, either by the game makers or someone else. She had a silver ring in one nostril which seemed to sparkle in the bright lights. She was clearly scared, her lips quivering, her eyes wide, but she stood straight, facing whatever was to come with fire in her eyes.

Something about her felt familiar. The longer I stared at her, the more I felt it.

But it couldn't be.

I forced myself to resume the broadcast, averting my eyes out of respect when the cameras zoomed in on her naked body. Perverts, all of them. There was no reason not to give her clothes. They wouldn't offer her any protection from the dangers of Kalumbu, but at least she'd have her dignity. Even coming from a species that only put on a loincloth when in contact with aliens, I knew that Peritans treasured being covered. Penny had explained it to me when she'd first arrived on the Artep. And the game makers had to know it. It was yet another way of how they manipulated their contestants, making them feel vulnerable before they even set foot on Kalumbu.

Kalumbu, the planet of death. Only two people had ever survived the Trials and they were on board the Artep just now. Other contestants had won the Trials, which was achieved after staying alive for ten days, but we'd discovered quickly that their supposed success didn't last long. They were killed as soon as the cameras were turned off. Nobody had left Kalumbu alive until Fay and Vruhag.

The game makers had already tightened their security since I'd hacked their systems. Rescuing the female wouldn't be as easy as it had been with the orc and his mate. I'd have to find another way to break through the shields they kept around the planet, preventing anyone from flying to the surface or beaming them up into orbit. It had worked last time because they hadn't expected anyone to try.

I focused back on the screen. Raucous applause sounded when the platform the female stood on began to move. She was about to be transported down onto the surface of Kalumbu. She wouldn't last long there. Fay had help from a native species, but what were the chances that the same would happen for this female? No, it was on me to get her out. I had to find a way to hack the systems and fast. Every click that passed could be the one that brought her death.

The camera focused on her face again. All traces of fear had vanished, leaving only cold determination. She seemed to look right at me, her amber eyes dark with defiance, and that's when I knew.

My hearts skipped a beat.

She was mine.

My atm. My mate.

The world seemed to hold its breath. My mate was about to be sent to Kalumbu. I had to save her, no matter the cost. This was no longer just a rescue mission for a random female.

She meant the universe to me.

"I swear on the Horned God that I will save you or die trying," I whispered and pricked my thumbs at the tips of my horns. I smeared the blood over my horns, sealing the oath.

I stared into her amber eyes. "I will come for you."

This series continues in My Big Furry Alien Satyr.

Want to find out how Penny and Qong met? Read My Big Sweet Waffle Monster for free by signing up to my newsletter:
https://skyemackinnon.com/wafflemonster

If you enjoyed this book, please take a moment to leave a review.

STARLIGHT MONSTERS BOOK 2
MY BIG FURRY ALIEN SATYR
USA TODAY BESTSELLING AUTHOR
SKYE MACKINNON

ACKNOWLEDGMENTS

Dear readers,

I very much hope you enjoyed this book. As soon as I saw this cover by the extremely talented Sanja Gombar, I knew I had to write a story for this orc. As so often, it's turned into a series, with a satyr and a naga next in line.

As much as I despaired at how Vruhag and Fay refused to find each other (eleven chapters, seriously?!), I enjoyed exploring Kalumbu with them. The chii were never supposed to exist - I'd planned the planet as a completely hostile place with no friendly species - but when Chirpy appeared, she brought with her an entire clan. I had great fun with their antics and can assure you that they're safe from the evil game makers.

As always, a huge thanks goes to my fellow Flockies Arizona, Laura and Kelly, who are my bouncing balls for ideas and never seem to get tired of my random ramblings. The same goes for my assistant Tricia, who's the brains behind the operations and who makes sure my newsletter gets sent on the right day and with the right content. And my beta reader Tory, who zipped through this book and was the first person to fall in love with the chii.

My family watch from afar, amused and slightly horrified at what I write, but I thank them anyway for their support. The same goes for my lovely non-author friends who stop me from being a complete hermit.

And the final thank you goes to my cat Sootie, for not throwing up on the keyboard, for not biting the computer cables, for not deleting my entire manuscript, for being the cutest and most loving cat ever.

Happy reading,
Skye

THE STARLIGHT UNIVERSE

This book is part of the Starlight Universe, an entire galaxy filled with hunky aliens, exotic planets, and the human women ready to find love among the stars.

Starlight Highlanders Mail Order Brides

Alien Highlanders in kilts come to Earth in search of brides... and take them to planet Albya. Three m/f standalones full of humour, action and steamy romance. Part of the Intergalactic Dating Agency.

The Intergalactic Guide to Humans

A humorous take on alien abductions, probing and other shenanigans. One reverse harem trilogy about clueless aliens and the human woman they abducted, followed by several standalone romances with various pairings (m/f, f/m/f and m/m). If you want light entertainment filled with unicorns, fabulous misunderstandings and unusual body parts, this is the series for you.

Starlight Vikings

Set on Earth and on the spaceship Valkyr, this trilogy of m/f standalones is all about hunky alien Vikings in need of females. Part of the Intergalactic Dating Agency.

Starlight Monsters

These aliens are not your usual humanoids... they have claws, fangs, tails, scales, knotty dicks and will growl at you. Interconnected m/f standalones with lots of action, steam and fated mates.

ABOUT THE AUTHOR

Skye MacKinnon is a USA Today & International Bestselling Author whose books are filled with strong heroines who don't have to choose.

She embraces her Scottishness with fantastical Scottish settings and a dash of mythology, no matter if she's writing about Celtic gods, aliens, cat shifters, or the streets of Edinburgh.

When she's not typing away at her favourite cafe, Skye loves dried mango, as much exotic tea as she can squeeze into her cupboards, and being covered in pet hair by her tiny black cat.

Subscribe to her newsletter:
skyemackinnon.com/newsletter

Find all of Skye's sci-fi romance in one place:
skyemackinnon.com/scifi

ALSO BY

Find all of Skye's books on her website, skyemackinnon.com, where you can also order signed paperbacks and swag.

Many of her books are available as audiobooks.

SCIENCE FICTION ROMANCE

Set in the Starlight Universe

- **Starlight Vikings** (sci-fi m/f romance, part of the Intergalactic Dating Agency)
- **Starlight Monsters** (sci-fi m/f romance)
- **Starlight Highlanders Mail Order Brides** (sci-fi m/f romance, part of the Intergalactic Dating Agency)
- **The Intergalactic Guide to Humans** (sci-fi romance with various pairings)

Set in other worlds

- **Between Rebels** (sci-fi reverse harem set in the Planet Athion shared world)
- **The Mars Diaries** (sci-fi reverse harem)
- **Aliens and Animals** (f/f sci-fi romance co-written with Arizona Tape)

- **Through the Gates** (dystopian reverse harem co-written with Rebecca Royce)

PARANORMAL & FANTASY ROMANCE

- **Claiming Her Bears** (post-apocalyptic shifter reverse harem)
- **Daughter of Winter** (fantasy reverse harem)
- **Catnip Assassins** (urban fantasy reverse harem)
- **Infernal Descent** (paranormal reverse harem based on Dante's Inferno, co-written with Bea Paige)
- **Seven Wardens** (fantasy reverse harem co-written with Laura Greenwood)
- **The Lost Siren** (post-apocalyptic, paranormal reverse harem co-written with Liza Street)

OTHER SERIES

- **Academy of Time** (time travel academy standalones, reverse harem and m/f)
- **Defiance** (contemporary reverse harem with a hint of thriller/suspense)

STANDALONES

- Song of Souls – m/f fantasy romance, fairy tale retelling
- Their Hybrid – steampunk reverse harem
- Partridge in the P.E.A.R. - sci-fi reverse harem co-written with Arizona Tape
- Highland Butterflies – lesbian romance

ANTHOLOGIES AND BOX SETS

- Hungry for More – charity cookbook
- Daggers & Destiny – a Skye MacKinnon starter library

Printed in Great Britain
by Amazon